TWO WEEKS

In

Chestertown

Brooke Martin

To my mom & my Great Grandfather Bud - Thank you for inspiring this story to fruition. How beautiful it is to be forever intertwined by the creative current that runs so deeply within us. Thank you both for paving the way...

AVA

They say you tend to remember every detail about a day like that day. Down to the minute. I only remember the smell. My hospital room had a vase of bright yellow sunflowers on the windowsill.

To this day, I can't smell sunflowers without puking.

The nurses were crying. Everyone around me was crying. I wasn't even crying. I remember how embarrassed I felt that I couldn't produce one single tear. Not one tear when a nameless social worker crouched down over my hospital bed and told me my parents were killed on impact in a car accident. I blamed my dad. He was always taking those switchbacks a bit too fast.

My parents left me no will. That's so typical of them. Never the planners. Always the eternal optimists. There's not much to be optimistic about when you're dead, is there, Mom? The nameless social worker with bad breath told me

I was a property of the state. I thought the state was a

person. I was looking forward to meeting them. Little did I

know the foster system would be less than thrilled to meet

me.

———————

Ava leans over the thick slab of Calcutta marble that

drapes her countertops. She's in baby blue silk pajamas,

sipping on an Oat Latte.

People are always telling her blue is her color because it

brings out her eyes. Her dark, ocean-blue eyes.

She freezes when she spots a vase of sunflowers

sitting next to the kitchen window.

Those were not there last night, she thinks.

She heads to the sink and pours out her freshly

brewed latte. Nausea is churning inside her stomach. All

she can taste now is bitterness. Ava grabs the vase of

sunflowers and discards them into the trash.

Much better, she thinks.

She plops down on one of her overpriced Serena & Lilly barstool chairs and scrolls aimlessly through her phone.

Hungry Heart by Bruce Springsteen starts to play through the kitchen Sonos speakers.

Her husband is awake, clearly.

As if on cue, Max Greenfield strolls into the kitchen, bedhead and all. At 6'4", he is hard to miss. He's boyishly cute in his green-striped boxer briefs.

Ava stares at him in amusement. She's always loved his zest for life. He appreciates the little things, while she always seems caught up in the perpetual anxiety of things that have not yet happened. However, there's not too much to worry about when you're born into one of the wealthiest families in London. Max has always had the upper hand in life, even from the womb. He's London royalty sans the title and crown. You would never know it by looking at him, though. His shaggy brown hair and baggy Levi jeans

he's had a pension for wearing every day since Ava met

him make him seem like he'd blend right in at the local

pub.

"C'mon Ava, how can you be sad when you get to

wake up to the boss!?" Max says, smirking.

Ava pulls her husband into her and gives him a slow

kiss. "You're absolutely mad, but I love you for it."

She puts an everything bagel in the toaster oven and

powers off the speaker. "I love Bruce, but I need absolute

silence to prepare for my meeting."

Max rolls his eyes as he starts up the fancy Sonic

Power Espresso machine. "Babe, you've been over your

presentation fifty-plus times. You've got this in the bag,

doll."

Doll. Ava loves it when Max calls her that. It's one

of the reasons she moved to London all those years ago.

The Brits have such a sophisticated way of speaking. Quite

the opposite from the Eastern Shore drawl she grew up with.

"This is the biggest bid Archer Architects has ever done. If we win, this could revolutionize the London tube," Ava is in full business mode now. " Shit, this would flip the transportation industry completely on it's ass."

Max throws up his hands in defeat. This is a road he does not want to go down with Ava. By the looks of it, it's a road he's been down far too many times.

He grabs the whole milk from the fridge and gives it a sniff, "Phew! How long has this thing been in here?"

"You're the only one who drinks that poison," Ava replies without looking up from her phone.

Ever since her parent's death, Ava has been obsessed with clean eating. That first year after the accident, she lost so much weight you could see every rib poking out from her bony torso.

Max prances around the kitchen with a pinky pointed up on his coffee mug. "Excuse me, Miss, I don't drink whole milk because I don't need it, and it's terrible for your immune system. Blah Blah Blah."

Ava rolls her eyes at his mockery. Max tosses out the soiled milk in the trashcan.

"Hey! My flowers!"

"Oh, sorry! I guess I forgot to tell you that I'm allergic to sunflowers," Ava swallows hard. She prays Max won't press her on this.

There is a long pause in the room as Max thinks this over.

Finally, he hunches over the countertop in a fit of laughter. "So typical. I buy my girl flowers for the first time, and I get it bloody wrong!"

Max is still laughing as he takes his plate and coffee and heads for the kitchen table. Through sloppy bites, he mumbles, "Fuck sunflowers, huh?"

"Fuck sunflowers," Ava says a bit too aggressively.

You have no idea, Max. No idea, Ava thinks.

––––––––––––

Ava is wearing a pale pink knee-length dress paired perfectly with a cream blazer. She stands before a group of male executives seated around an oval table.

If exclusivity had a smell, it would wreak throughout this entire room of big hitters.

Ava straightens her blazer. "London transportation will only get busier. We have the unique opportunity to reshape how the world thinks about the transportation industry. Our zero-carbon design is the first of its kind and can reduce our carbon footprint by almost eighty-two percent."

A coworker once accused Ava of being neurotically obsessed with climate change. If that's Ava's worst flaw, she's completely fine with it. It's one of the other obsessions Ava picked up after her parent's death. She would frequently spend hours at night thinking about the legacy her parents left behind and what kind of legacy she wanted to leave behind. She made a vow to herself that she would do everything she could to leave this place better than she found it. That's why she chose Archer Architects. She didn't want to work at just any architectural firm. She wanted to work at a revolutionary firm that was one hundred percent eco-friendly.

A grey-haired man stands up. His stonelike expression accentuates every fine wrinkle on his forehead. "Well, Ava, you and your team have given us plenty to consider. Well done. We'll be in touch."

Ava gives him a soft smile. The look in her eyes suggests she's determined to win him over. She's not letting him off the hook that easily. A meticulously worded follow-up email will be in his inbox within the hour.

Once the testosterone group of big hitters exits the room, Ava turns to her other female coworker, Betsy Walters. Betsy lets out a sigh of relief.

"Sheesh. Tough crowd. They don't give away too much, do they?" Betsy says.

Ava leans back in her swivel chair, "I think we've got them. The price tag was a bit of a shocker at first, but they know it's necessary. We can't cut corners on this. Not unless we want the EPA cock blocking us every step of the way."

Both Ava and Betsy let out a strained sigh. This project has been three years in the making. Ava's given everything she has to it. She won't allow it to go South; too much is on the line.

The Archer Architects receptionist pokes her head into the room.

"Ava, someone from Thompkins Bay Law Firm is on the phone asking for you. He's been quite persistent."

Ava gives her a confused look, "Christ, we're already being sued for our designs!? The project hasn't even started yet!"

Betsy stands up and grabs her stack of papers. "Bring on the haters!"

She exits the room just as the receptionist patches the call through to Ava.

Ava lets the phone ring twice before picking up.

"This is Ava Greenfield."

A man with a raspy voice is on the other end of the line, "Ava! I'm glad I finally got ahold of you! You're one tough cookie to reach. My name is Sam Thompkins. I'm one of the attorneys for Thompkins Bay Law Firm."

Ava looks annoyed as she places her blazer on the backseat of her chair. Her slender arms suggest she's a regular at pilates or some ritzy, overpriced exercise class. "Thompkins Bay Law Firm? Where is that?"

"We're located in Chestertown, Maryland. We represent clients all across the Maryland seaboard."

Ava's face goes stark white at the mention of Chestertown, Maryland.

"Maryland? I'm sorry, you must have the wrong person," Ava visibly winces as she says Maryland. "I don't live in Maryland."

Anymore, she thinks.

Ava can hear the man on the other end of the line shuffling a stack of papers. "You are Ava Greenfield, correct? Your maiden name is Ava McGready. Your parents were Donna and Jeff McGready, correct?"

Ava stands up from her chair, "I'm sorry – what is this about?"

It's been so long since she heard her parent's names. If she's being honest, it's been so long since she's thought about her parents at all.

"Well, we were clearing out an attorney's desk at our firm who recently passed away. Mr. Gerold Finley. Does that name ring a bell?"

"I'm afraid not," Ava replies curtly.

"Well, sorting through his papers, we found your file. Specifically, your will."

Ava semi-laughs, "Okay, this must be a mistake. My parents left me no will."

Sam clears his throat, "I hate to be the one telling you this over the phone, but your parents did indeed have a will written up for you. Mr. Finley withheld the papers, for whatever reason, leaving us all to assume you were left without a will."

"Wait. What? What are you trying to say?" Ava sits back down and places her hands firmly on the boardroom table. She needs to steady herself. "I don't understand."

She does not have time for this. She needs to send a carefully worded follow-up email ASAP. Timing is everything in her business.

"Rest assured, we are doing everything possible to correct these mistakes. Our only goal is to restore what is rightfully yours. Free of charge, of course."

"Is this a scam!?"

"No, it's not a scam. Again, I hate to do this over the phone. Is there any way you can come into our office? The biggest item on your will is the property with the address listed as 1211 Happy Hollow Road."

1211. Those four numbers are still the passcode for all her apps and banking information. She could never forget those four numbers if she tried.

Ava can barely speak, "My parent's house?"

"Yes. Your parents will clearly state that if something happened to them, you rightfully become the owner of this property."

"I haven't been to that property since my parents died. Is it even still standing?" Ava asks.

"Very much so. As you know, it's situated on a coveted corner of the Chesapeake Bay. Water properties like this are selling at a minimum of three million today. Give or take."

Ava laughs, "Three million? Now I know this is a scam. Please don't call back here again."

Sam is utterly desperate now, "Wait! Does Ako ring a bell? The will was made out to Little Miss Ako."

Ava's blood runs cold. That name. It holds so much weight, even to this day.

"Are you still there?" Sam asks.

"No. It does not ring a bell. Please don't call here again." Ava ends the call and looks down at her perfectly manicured hands. They're trembling, and it's not just because she's on her third coffee of the day, and it's not even noon.

Ava rushes out of the boardroom to find Betsy. She's hunkered down in her cubicle, berating the keyboard with her fingers.

"Betz, can you do me a favor and send the follow-up email and the recap notes?" Ava grabs her stomach, "I'm not feeling great. I'm going to work the rest of the day from home."

Betsy nods but gives Ava a concerned look.

"I'll be fine. Just need a bit of rest." Ava does her best to reassure her. "See you bright and early tomorrow!"

Betsy looks far from reassured. It's unlike Ava to call out for a sick day. Ava landed Archer Architect's first seven-figure deal, all while battling strep throat and a double ear infection. Pain has always been something Ava can push through. This is a different kind of pain, though. A pain Ava has been running from for a long, long time. She's not going to let it catch up to her. Not now, after all these years.

———————————

It's Eleven P.M. London time, and Max is fast asleep in the other room. Ava sits next to a half-drunken bottle of Cabernet Sauvignon. Her computer screen illuminates a soft yellow light.

On the computer screen, there's an image of the Thompkins Bay Law Firm logo. Ava scrolls a bit further down the page to see a photo of a man who appears to be in his late fifties with jet-black hair. Next to his picture reads his name: Sam Thompkins.

She takes a slug directly from the wine bottle.

Ava continues scrolling until she finds the 'Contact Us' section. Her mouse hovers over the number.

She grabs her phone and dials the number before she can convince herself otherwise. Someone picks up on the third ring.

"Sam? Hello?" Ava's voice is shaky, "Is this Sam Thompkins?"

"Ava. I was hoping you'd call me back," Sam sounds tired yet relieved.

"If I fly all the way to Maryland and come to see you, will I be meeting you or a serial killer waiting to stab me to death?" Ava's getting right to the point. She's oblivious to the fact that it's earlier than five AM on the East Coast.

Sam lets out a loud, croaky laugh. "Sweetie, Chestertown is twelve miles long and eight miles wide. Everyone knows everyone. A serial killer wouldn't last a damn minute in this town."

"Okay then. I'll see you tomorrow afternoon."

Ava hangs up before Sam can respond. She lets out the breath she's been unknowingly holding since this afternoon when she received the call from Sam.

———————

It's very early London time. The sun has yet to rise in the posh neighborhood of South Kensington.

Ava is zipping up her suitcase and checking her purse for her ID and earbuds. Max hovers over his wife like a linebacker waiting for his next tackle. "Babe, you have to admit this sounds absolutely nuts."

"Max, don't you think I know this? Don't you think I've been over every freaking scenario in my mind!?" Ava snaps back.

"So explain to me why the hell you're still packing your luggage and going?"

"I can't explain it. In a way that will make sense, at least." Ava grabs her cashmere duster sweater from the hall closet. "I just have to see it with my own eyes. The house. The will."

Max continues to pace the entryway hallway.

"Ava, this is 2018. If there was a 'said' will, don't you think he could send it over electronically?"

Ava ignores him.

Max cups Ava's cheeks in both his hands. "Babe, I don't think you're thinking clearly."

She gives him a feigned smile, "I need to tie up these loose ends. I need to finally put my past to rest."

While Max knows a fair amount about Ava's past, he isn't privy to the nitty gritty details, like the fact that she absolutely hates sunflowers. Ava has been reluctant to share everything with him because there was no point in revealing it all. It wouldn't change the past.

Max sighs. He knows his wife better than anyone. Just like he knows that when Ava gets her mind set on something she's like a dog with a bone.

"Please keep your phone on you at all times and share your location with me. If anything, ANYTHING seems sketchy or does not feel right, get the hell out of there. Do you hear me?"

Ava is fishing around in her purse for her car keys but keeps coming up empty-handed.

"Ava! Do you hear me?" Max repeats himself, a bit louder this time.

Ava snaps to, "Yes. Of course. I love you, Max. I'll be safe, I promise. Just a few days and then I'll be back like I never left!"

She tries to sound convincing, but her voice has the slightest hint of doubt.

Ava gives Max one last kiss and throws her purse over her shoulder. She calls for the elevator as Max stands territorially by the door. She gives him one last reassuring look before she descends down the elevator and into the thick morning fog

———————

Thirty thousand feet in the air and sound asleep, the dream returns to Ava all too easily. She's five years old, watching her father pull the oyster trap out of the water. Her father's dirty hand flips open the oyster trap. He always had a thick line of dirt underneath each fingernail. He liked to say it was a sign of a hard day's work. The more dirt under your nails, the harder you must have worked.

"Alright, Ava. Hand me your best pick." Ava's father says.

Ava has an elated smile on her face. She picks up one of the oysters in the trap, weighing it in her hands. "No! This one." She picks up another oyster with a jagged, diamond-like shape. It's small and underrated.

"That's the one you want?" Ava's father asks.

She nods her head yes and watches as her father slowly pries the oyster open.

"My gosh. Do you know what this is? This is an Akoya pearl oyster. One of the hardest and rarest to find out here." Her father hands her the opened oyster, "Look at the pearl inside."

Ava's eyes light up as she sees the lone pearl lying perfectly in the middle of the shell. She smiles so big that the gap in her two front teeth takes up half her face.

"Go on and grab it. It's yours to keep. What do you think about that, little Miss Ako?"

"Excuse me."

Ava is jolted from her dream. Her plane passenger is shaking her leg.

"Excuse me. I have to use the restroom."

Ava scoots aside to let them pass. She intuitively grabs at the pearl necklace hanging from her collarbone as she checks the flight map. Two more hours until touchdown. She closes her eyes again, begging to be transported back into the dream.

WEEK ONE

Ava parks her large SUV rental in the parking lot at the DoubleTree Hotel. It was either the DoubleTree or a motel with a recent bed bug infestation—slim pickings.

It took her two hours after landing to get to the tiny crabbing village that is Chestertown, Maryland. Every inch of Chestertown seems to be surrounded by the Chesapeake Bay. Even the local gas station has a picturesque view of the Bay.

It really is a beautiful backdrop. Too bad this entire place is soiled with rottenness, Ava thinks.

Ava gets out of the SUV, and the first thing she's hit with is the smell. A smell she knows all too well. Salt and brine mixed with a little bit of old bay. Home. Or what once was.

She reluctantly enters the entrance to the hotel. There's a line for check-in so she grabs her phone to text Max that she's landed safely. She's always forgetting to text people back. It's one of her shortcomings. It drives Max

crazy. Max, on the other hand, is glued to his phone. It

drives Ava crazy. Just once, she would love to have a

dinner out with Max where he wasn't whipping out his

phone every time one of his favorite teams scored a goal.

Ava's lost in thought when she hears her name.

"Ava?"

Ava spins around. A thin, 5'2" brunette woman in a

housekeeping uniform is calling her name. "Ava, is that

you?"

"Hi, yes. I'm Ava. I'm sorry. Do I know you?"

The brunette's hair is pulled up into a messy bun.

Her uniform looks a bit worse for wear and she does not

seem to be wearing a bra.

"Holy shit! It is you!" The brunette pushes her

laundry cart to the side, enveloping Ava in a bear hug. For

her tiny size, she packs quite the punch.

"It's Lucy! Lucy Rodriguez."

Ava still looks confused. She's racking her brain, trying to register who this is.

"From Sister Catherine's foster home!"

Ava goes wide-eyed. "Holy moly. Lucy!?"

The brunette has a clown like smile smeared across her face.

"Oh my god. Lucy! I'm so sorry, you'll have to forgive me," Ava fishes around in her purse, "I don't have my glasses on."

Lucy waves her off, "I can't believe you're here! Wait, why are you here?"

"Well, I–" Ava stutters. She wasn't prepared to run into anyone, let alone have to explain why she is here, in Chestertown, Maryland, of all places, "I'm tying up loose ends on a few family matters that required me to be here in person."

Lucy smacks her lips, "Wow. I really can't believe you're here standing in front of me. How long has it been?"

The man working the front desk gives Lucy a look of warning.

Lucy flicks him off, "Fuck off, Jerry. I just cleaned puke out of room ten. I think I deserve a five-minute break."

Ava blushes with embarrassment. She can't believe Lucy said that out loud in front of a crowd of customers.

"I should get back to it before Jerry has a conniption. But, hey, do you want to grab a bite later and catch up?" Lucy asks.

"Oh, I had an early flight. I planned on grabbing a quick bite at Lucille's and calling it early tonight."

Lucy is grinning, "Shit, you really haven't been back here since you left, huh?"

Ava shifts uncomfortably from one foot to another. She really should have worn more sensible shoes. Her Dolce Vita heels make her stick out like a sore thumb in this place.

Lucy continues, "Lucille's has been closed for over a decade. Let me take you to Brophy's Oyster House. It's new and relatively decent for this town, which isn't saying much."

Ava has never been any good at saying no. She can't count the amount of uncomfortable situations she's gotten herself into because she can't be an asshole. Max would have told her to buzz off all too easily. For as nice as Max seems, he has a mean streak that, when activated, can be quite terrifying. The first time Ava saw it come out, she didn't talk to Max for a full week. They were waiting for the tube after a Tottenham Hotspurs game when a beggar came up to them and asked for some money. After they declined, the beggar kept asking quite persistently. After the third time, Max got right into the beggar's face and growled at him to "Fuck off, or else." It caused quite the scene. Ava couldn't believe Max had taken it to that level of aggression all over a poor man trying to get a few pounds for food. Ava swore she would never speak to Max again if he ever pulled that stunt again. For the most part, Max has done a good job of keeping this mean streak at bay. That doesn't mean Ava isn't always on edge, though. She's always waiting for the moment when she needs to step in and diffuse the situation. Max's gregarious and chivalrous personality seems to mask any faults that lie beneath the surface. But Ava is not one to forget. She's always ready. Her childhood taught her that. The minute you let your guard down is the minute you get pounced on.

"Ava?" Lucy is standing in front of Ava, waiting for an answer.

"Sure. Would love to catch up."

"Great! I'll pick you up here around five. It's casual dining, so don't go breaking out your fanciest Crocs for this." Lucy looks down at Ava's heels with the slightest hint of judgment.

They both smile. There is a moment where they almost communicate something unspoken with their eyes, but the moment quickly passes.

Lucy peels off down the hallway with her bulky cart, leaving Ava feeling like she's just stepped into the twilight zone.

––––––––––

Ava sits across from Sam Thompkins as he shuffles through a large stack of papers. His desk is filled with documents strewn every which way. Organized chaos, one could say. A complete shitshow is what Ava would call it. He's shorter than Ava expected. She may even be an inch or two taller than him, especially in her heels. Again, Ava regrets her shoe choice. She's clearly out of place in the tiny shack that is Thompkins Bay Law Firm.

"Ah! Here it is!" Sam produces a manilla folder with Ava McGready written on it in thick Sharpie. Ava cringes at the sight of her maiden name. Sam slides the folder across the table.

She looks down at the unopened folder. Ava starts to have a queasy feeling, as if what she's about to open is somehow a trap door to her past.

"I went through every file in that folder thrice times over. It clearly states several times that you are the rightful and lawful owner of the 1211 Happy Hollow estate."

Ava scoffs, "Ha, I wouldn't exactly call it an estate."

Sam looks at Ava with a hint of sadness behind his dark brown eyes. "Can I get you a coffee?"

Ava waves him off. Her eyes are laser-focused on the folder. Ava is strictly business today.

"Now, if you flip to page twelve, you will see your name listed as the sole beneficiary of 1211 Happy Hollow Road. I almost chucked this folder out while cleaning through Gerold's desk. Thank goodness I didn't."

Ava shakes her head. She's not understanding, "I'm confused. So you're telling me this Gerold guy at your firm was my parent's attorney, and he supposedly lost the will after they died?"

"He didn't 'supposedly'. He did lose the will. For whatever reason, none of us will know. We can't exactly ask him from six feet under, can we?" Sam lets out a chuckle but quickly stops himself as he notices Ava's very stern demeanor across the table. She's not amused by any of this.

"Please, take your time going through the folder. I can give you all the time you need, Miss McGready." Sam continues.

"It's Mrs. Greenfield. Please call me Mrs. Greenfield."

"I apologize, Mrs. Greenfield. You can call me Sam."

"Sam," Ava repeats, "I'm sorry, but I don't have much time to go through this entire stack. Can you just tell me what I need to do? What papers do I need to sign?"

Sam clears his throat. He sits up a bit straighter. He nervously combs his fingers through his graying mustache. "I wish it were that easy. You see, Maryland laws make it extra difficult to grant the paperwork needed to have a squatter vacate a property."

"A squatter?"Ava looks at Sam as if he has five heads, "What do you mean a squatter?"

"Oh! I guess I left that out on our call. I'm sorry. This has been a whirlwind of developments. I'm doing my very best to keep everyone abreast as I become privy to all the information."

"Sam?" Ava has no time for Sam's tongue-tied rambling explanation. She just wants him to get to the point.

Sam clarifies, "There seems to be a squatter on the property."

Ava looks relieved, "Oh. Well, we will just tell them to leave. This paperwork should be more than enough proof of ownership."

Sam gets up from his desk and closes the door. Ava does not like the tone of where this conversation is going. "This squatter – this woman – she seems to be adamant that she has the documents to prove her legal residency of the estate."

"What the hell!" Ava's demeanor has turned from annoyance to sheer anger.

Sam is a bit taken aback by Ava's sharp change of tone.

"I'm sorry for my bluntness," Ava continues, " But you have to understand that I flew here to sign a few papers and have this whole thing wrapped up in a day. I did not come here to settle some sort of land dispute. Especially a land I had no idea I even owned until a day ago!"

Sam continues, trying his best to redirect this conversation back to a calming place. "Our records indicate this property is worth upwards of three million dollars. That's a large sum of money that we want to return to you rightfully. Again, at no cost to you for our services."

"It's not about the money! I have money."

"Mrs. Greenfield…" Sam looks terrified.

"I mean, how did this happen? How did you lose my will?" Ava holds up the folder with authority. "This was my entire childhood! Gone. Erased."

Ava's eyes start to well up with tears. She will not let herself break down in the middle of this low-budget law office. She's stronger than this. She slowly counts in her head, one…two…

She collects herself, "I'm sorry, Sam. I know it's not your fault. I know you didn't do this. I just want to get this all over with so I can go home. To London, I mean. My home."

"I completely understand," Sam pats her shoulder, "You can trust me. I will make sure we right this wrong. You have my word."

A few silent moments pass by.

Ava is visibly weighing her options. She could just return to London and forget she ever received a call from Sam Thompkins. She could press charges against this squatter, take her to court, and let the law handle this. But what has the law done for her besides just let her down? No, she will handle this herself. She's Ava Greenfield. She gets shit done, and this will be no exception.

"I'm going to go have a chat with the squatter," Ava says as she collects her coat and sticks the manilla folder deep within her purse.

Sam stands up, looking very flummoxed, "Oh! Mrs.

Greenfield, I really don't recommend that. Please give us a

few days, and I will try my best to expedite this process."

Ava smiles softly at Sam. He seems like such a nice

man who seems to be all too ready for retirement. I bet he

didn't see this wrench in his plans. "Thank you, but I don't

exactly have time for the run-around. I'll handle it, Sam.

I'll keep you posted on how the chat goes."

Without another word, Ava glides out of the office.

The clacking of her heels against the parking lot pavement

seems to echo like a warning across the entire town.

———————

Ava makes a sharp right turn that leads her onto a

no-name gravel road. Weeds and brush have all but taken

over this pothole-riddled road. She parks her car in front of

a rusted iron gate. She has no memory of that gate ever

being there. Then again, she was just seven years old when

her parents died. It's been over twenty years since she's stepped foot onto this property.

She creaks open the gate and seems to enter a parallel universe.

She's first struck by the vastness of this piece of property. The house itself, beaten and falling apart, is just a little speck on the corner of this massive land. She spots the dock, or what's left of it. A dock that leads to the all-encompassing panoramic and unobstructed view of the Chesapeake Bay. She understands why this property would go for millions of dollars. How quickly she forgot about this view. This million-dollar view. Her million-dollar view, apparently.

While Max and Ava aren't exactly strapped for cash, a few million in the bank would be nice. She's been wanting to break away from Archer Architects and finally start her own firm. Plus, the fertility issues have really started to make a large dent in their once hefty savings. Ava knows they can always lean on Max's parents if the money gets tight, but she also knows Max would never succumb to that level. He's far too prideful to let it get to that point.

Ava's attention is brought back to the dock. How often would she sit on that dock with her parents and watch the sunrise? She's always been an early riser, even to this day. Something about being the first person to see the world come to life has always enthralled her.

Off to the left is an old wooden barn. From what Ava can remember, they never did have any animals living in that barn. The barn was simply a great hiding spot for a game of hide and seek or the home to an old tire swing. She wonders if that swing is still there.

Ava inches closer toward the pastel yellow door. Its paint is chipped, and the frame on the door is slowly shifting to the right. It would be so easy for someone to break in. This is technically her house, after all.

She glances at the tree stump that sits right next to the yellow door.

A memory rushes in before she can stop it. Ava's wearing a ballerina tutu and sitting cross-legged beside the tree stump. Across from her is her mother, smiling from ear to ear. Her mother's strawberry blonde hair blows gently from the wind off the bay.

"Remember, ladies chew with their mouth closed." Her mother says as she takes one large bite of a croissant and chews it with her mouth wide open. Crumbs fall everywhere.

Little Ava can't contain her laughter, "Tell me more about London, Mama."

Her mother's eyes light up, "Oh, you would love London! It's moody and dramatic but also beautifully bright and cheery. My mother used to take me for a spot of tea every Sunday, and we would dress up in our Sunday best. I'll show you London one day when you're old enough. We'll have a proper English tea party. What do you think about that?"

"Who the fuck are you?"

Ava is jolted back to reality.

A tall, stick-thin blonde is leaning up against the yellow door. The blonde looks almost sickly.

Ava is so taken aback that she can't seem to produce a single word. She was not expecting this blonde figure. She was expecting an unassuming older woman whom she would have to kindly escort off the property. This blonde looks scrappy and wild, like a child of the woods.

"Hello? I said who are you?" The blonde hisses again.

"My name is Ava. Ava Greenfield," Ava sticks out her hand but quickly retracts it once she realizes how silly formalities are in this scenario.

The blonde is almost snarling at Ava. "Can I help you? This is private property."

"Ah," Ava digs in her purse for the paperwork, "That's kind of why I'm here. Well, that's really the only reason why I'm here. To discuss this property."

The blonde's raccoon eyes grow even darker. "Yes?"

Ava hands over the papers.

A long silence passes as the blonde takes her time reading through the first page of the will.

Off in the distance, a crane glides slowly across the water. Crane's were always Ava's favorite. Something about their long sleek legs and plier-like beaks have always fascinated her. She really has entered into another world.

The blonde starts ripping up the papers.

"What are you doing!?" Ava asks.

She throws the papers in Ava's face, "Get the fuck out of here."

Ava has a chill run down her spine.

"You legally do not own this house. You have to vacate the property immediately!" Ava's voice is shaking, making things that much worse for her.

The blonde steps closer so she's face to face with Ava. She's less than a foot away as she sticks out her arms and gives Ava a hard shove.

Ava stutters back but remains on her feet. She's stunned. This creature has just physically assaulted her. She'll sue. Can she sue? She's sure she can.

Ava takes a deep breath and counts to three. It's a technique she learned in her childhood therapy sessions when she felt like she was going to start crying. Since her parent's funeral, she has yet to shed one single tear. Not one when her college boyfriend, Jack, left her for her best friend. Not even one when she was twenty-two and got evicted from her shoebox London apartment when she couldn't make rent. Tears are a weakness and Ava has spent her entire adulthood proving she's anything but weak.

"Fine. You want to do this the hard way?" Ava's voice is now strong and firm. She's regained her composure, "I didn't want to get lawyers involved, but now you've left me no choice."

Ava starts walking towards the gated entrance. She turns back around before she's out of earshot, "You'll be out of here by tomorrow, so you'd better start packing, sweetie!"

Without another word, Ava climbs into her rental car and backs the car up with full force. Dust flies everywhere as the blonde is left watching Ava hightail it out of Happy Hollow Road.

————————

Ava and Lucy sit across from one another on the deck of Brophy's Oyster House. There's not much to write home about inside the restaurant, but the view of the Bay from the outside deck is the true masterpiece. The money shot. That's kind of the general theme for most of Chestertown, if not all of Chestertown. If it weren't for the Chesapeake Bay, this place would indeed be a no-name town.

Lucy has changed out of her uniform and is now sporting low-rise jeans and a silk tank top. She's quite curvacious, and her boobs seem to want to pop right out of her tank top. Ava finds it hard not to judge her outfit choice. She reminds herself she's not in London anymore, as if she could ever forget.

"What does your husband do?" Lucy asks. She's already downed her first margarita.

She told Ava this spot has the best margaritas in town. It sounded odd for a seafood joint, but Ava chose to give it a whirl.

"He's a real estate developer," Ava takes a careful sip of her margarita. It's not half bad, she thinks.

"A real estate developer! Wow. That's big time!"

"It's actually how we met. On a job site." Ava admits. Although, she tells most people they met at a bar. In their industry, it's quite frowned upon to fraternize with clients, especially big-time developers like Max Greenfield. Max rose to his high-brow position at Greenfield Developers by way of nepotism. He does not exactly help his image by rolling into work hours late and taking frivolous lunch meetings. He's untouchable. It's a fact no one in the company, not even Max, can deny. Regardless, both she and Max agreed it would be best to fudge the truth just a bit. A tiny, harmless white lie.

"What a powerful pair!" Lucy says, "A real estate developer and a top-tier architect!"

Ava is about to take another sip of her margarita but pauses,. "How did you know I was an architect?"

Lucy blushes, "Oh, well…. shoot. This is quite embarrassing, huh?" Lucy is stumbling over her words. "I must admit, I looked you up online. Once I saw you earlier today at the hotel, I got curious and gave it a quick Google search. I'm so sorry for being nosy."

Lucy is now beet red.

Ava has second-hand embarrassment for her but tries her best to reassure Lucy, "Oh, it's totally fine. Seriously, don't worry about it. That's the beauty of the internet. You can find just about anything you're looking for, right?"

"Right," Lucy whispers.

Ava desperately wants to change the subject.

"What about you? What have you been up to?" If Ava's being honest, she Googled Lucy as soon as she ran into her this afternoon but found she's made no impression on the internet—at least not any Lucy Gonzalez of

Chestertown, Maryland. The internet seems to have been wiped clean of Lucy Gonzalez.

"Oh, you know – I work odd jobs here and there. Working at the DoubleTree was only supposed to be temporary, but anytime I try to give my notice, they bump my pay. They really don't want me to leave. I guess I'm the best employee they can get."

"It's a very nice hotel. I was a bit surprised." Ava blurts out.

Lucy looks a bit hurt by this statement.

Get it together, Ava thinks to herself.

"I – I didn't mean it like that. It's just… it's been so long since I've been back here. We didn't even have our own grocery store, let alone a hotel. I mean, when I lived here people would quite literally bargain for food and goods like we were living off some sort of reservation. "

Ava is laughing to herself like a crazy person.

Lucy nods politely but looks as if she does not take kindly to Ava's backhanded remarks about her town.

Those margaritas really seem to have gotten to Ava. Why is she so tipsy? She usually has a pretty strong tolerance. Her tolerance is actually what led to the biggest fight Max and Ava have ever gotten into. Their fertility doctor dared to suggest her drinking may be the cause for why her body can't seem to produce a single viable egg. Max was all too eager to jump on that bandwagon. By no means is Ava an alcoholic. Ava's life in London is surrounded by alcohol, so it's inevitable she's built up quite a tolerance. She can't exactly show up to a charity event and ask for water, can she? That would send their entire social circle into a tailspin of assumptions that would ultimately lead to the fake news that Ava is pregnant. Ava once ordered a Diet Coke at a polo match and had to spend the next hour assuring all the ladies she was, in fact, not with child. Little did they know, three nights before she actually found out she was pregnant. She hadn't even told Max yet. She miscarried a few days later, which made her even more grateful she didn't tell a soul about it.

"So, you said you're tying up loose ends. What in the world does that mean?" Lucy inquires, "It must be pretty important to have had you fly all the way here from London."

The will. How could Ava have forgotten about it? It was nice not to think about it for a few short moments.

Ava clears her throat, "Well, it's kind of a long story."

Lucy motions to the beautiful burnt orange-yellow sunset forming behind them, "The night is still young."

Ava clutches the pearl necklace that sits right in the middle of her collarbone. Her safety net. "Turns out my parents did leave me with a will. After all this time. After all these years."

"No way." Lucy sits up a bit straighter in her chair, "I can't believe it. After all these years!"

"Yeah, pretty wild, huh? It's like my entire childhood was ripped out of my hands with one letter. And now…" Ava swallows down another gulp of her margarita. She's lost in thought. All the 'what if' scenarios are scratching at the surface of her mind, begging to be let out. No, She can't think like that. She needs to focus on the present and wrap this all up. What she really needs is to get home to her husband. This is the longest Ava has ever been apart from Max. She doesn't like to be far from Max. Once, when Max left for a Stag party, Ava had so much anxiety that something would happen to him that she didn't eat for the entire four days he was gone. She knows her dependence on Max is probably not healthy, but it is what it is. Ava knows this is yet another trauma response from her parent's dying so young. You seem to be forever hardwired to think everyone you love will leave you.

Lucy seems to sense Ava's uneasiness. She flags down the waitress for the check.

"I know it's been a long day for you, and I'm sure you're quite jet-lagged. Let's get out of here and get you some rest."

Ava smiles. She's beyond appreciative for an out. Ava checks her phone. She has three missed calls from Max. She'll get to those tomorrow. It's too late to call him tonight. He'll understand. Plus, he will notice she's had a few drinks and shift from his concerned to judgmental tone. Ava really has no time to deal with that right now.

"Great. I'm exhausted," Ava places her black AMEX down on the table. "My treat."

Lucy politely tries to put her card into the pile, "Let's split it."

Ava swats her away, "No, it's my pleasure. It's really nice to catch up with an old acquaintance."

"Yes, it's been nice catching up with you," Lucy

replies with far less conviction. "Shall we?"

Lucy stands up and gives Ava that look again. It's

like she can burn a hole through Ava's third eye. Ava's

never been into yoga, but she knows enough to know that

your third eye is important. Ava looks away. She really

needs to get out of here.

Lucy leads Ava outside the restaurant and to her car.

Ava heads in the opposite direction of Lucy. "I'm

parked over ssshere!" Ava says, slurring her words.

"Let me give you a ride home." Lucy says, " The

cops in this town have nothing better to do than to hang

outside these bars waiting for their next DUI ticket."

Ava smiles. She has had more to drink than she

would like to admit. She knows she's not in any condition

to drive. Hasn't Lucy had the same amount to drink? Why

does she seem to be way more put together than her right

now? Man, she can really hold her alcohol. Impressive, Ava thinks.

Ava hops into the passenger seat of Lucy's old Honda. It smells like a nauseating combination of cigarettes and cleaning supplies.

Ava rolls down the window, trying her best to be as polite as possible. "Sorry, I get overheated quite easily. It's such a nice night tonight. The cool breeze feels so good!"

Lucy says nothing. She keeps her eyes laser-focused on the road ahead. The car is silent for a few minutes.

"Hold on! Stop! Stop the car!" Ava sits up pin straight in her seat.

"I'm sorry, what?" Lucy asks.

"Sister Catherine's! That's Sister Catherine's, right?" Ava is pointing frantically outside her window.

Lucy looks to her right out the passenger side window. "Yeah. That was it. I think it's now a halfway house or something like that."

Ava unbuckles her seatbelt and opens the car door. She looks up at the old Victorian-style boarding house.

Lucy follows her outside the car and stands next to her. They both look up at the house, almost in a trance.

"It looks just the same. You would think after all these years I wouldn't remember what it looked like, but how could I possibly forget those yellow stained glass windows?" Ava reminisces, "I used to look out those windows and really think the world was tinted yellow. I thought I was losing my mind."

Lucy is staring up at those yellow windows, still in a trance-like state.

"Maybe I really did lose my mind," Ava continues.

She turns to Lucy, a bit more serious now, "What did you actually do for Sister Catherine's? I remember you being almost like a big sister to all of us girls."

Now that Ava thinks about it, Lucy was probably at least ten to fifteen years older than her. Back then, she didn't really notice the age gap. Now, looking at Lucy with her crow's feet and graying black hair, she wonders how old Lucy really is.

"I really did whatever Sister Marie asked of me."

"Sister Marie scared the shit out of me." Ava scoffs.

Lucy laughs.

"Why the hell did you work here?" Ava presses, "I mean, surely you could have made a lot more money at one of the restaurants in town. Why did you want to work here, of all places?"

"It didn't pay much, but it was my way of giving back." Lucy says, "My mother wasn't around growing up, but I had someone who was like a mother figure to me when I was younger. I guess it was my way of paying it forward."

"Oh wow, I didn't know that."

Now that Ava's thinking about it, there's a lot that she does not know about Lucy.

They both seem to be lost in thought.

"Ava…" Lucy says. That look in her eyes suggest she wants to say so much more.

Ava needs to focus on why she's here. She needs to reclaim ownership of the house and get back to Max and her job in London. Most importantly, she needs to call Betsy in the morning to see where they are with the heavy hitters. If she fails on this project, she can kiss her hopes of starting her own gig goodbye. This project will put Ava Greenfield on the map; she's sure of it.

"Right. Well, I really should be getting home," Ava lets out a forced yawn. "I'm exhausted."

Lucy nods. She seems disappointed. They both re-enter the car, leaving the Victorian house in their rearview. You can still almost see the yellow tint reflecting off the windows as the Honda slowly pulls away.

———————————

LUCY

She shouldn't be here. It's been twenty-three years.

Why the hell is she back? She's ruining everything. She

always ruins everything. Like father, like daughter. She's

going on and on about her husband like he's some God-like

figure. Like I didn't know every detail already. Of course I

did. I'm an observer. But more than that, I'm diligent. As

Ava said it herself, you can find out just about anything on

the internet. And the way she chalked us up to an

'acquaintanceship'. How absolutely pompous of her. It's as

if she can't possibly admit to ever being closely associated

with me. One thing is clear, she's a sloppy drunk. I poured

half my drink out both times she went to the bathroom. I

had to be sharp. I couldn't let anything throw me off. I

already had a minor slip-up about her job. I think I

recovered quite gracefully. I've always been good at

thinking on my feet. If it weren't for that crackhead lawyer,

everything would be as it should be: In the past. I should have known better with Gerold. I should have handled it

myself. Now I know better. I will handle it. Just like I

always have to do.

AVA

It's five in the morning, and Ava is sucking in the bitter October saltwater air. Her mouth is starting to taste like pennies. She's five miles in and almost at Brophy's Oyster House.

Ava couldn't sleep last night. She finally gave up on any hope of a good night's rest once the flood of memories from Sister Catherine's foster home came in fast and furious. Sister Catherine's was the keeper of her childhood for eleven years until she turned eighteen and booked the first one-way flight to London she could afford. At first, the orphanage was somewhat of a safe haven for Ava. After the shock of her parent's death subsided and reality took a firm hold, Ava felt comforted by the fact that she was surrounded by other girls just like her: poor and parentless. Ava quickly learned that the foster care system was merely a carefully constructed mechanism for a really good tax break. Everyone in the foster home was beyond miserable. There was no love to be spread around. Lucy Gonzalez was a pillar of stability for Ava during her adolescent years. Ava went to Lucy for just about anything and everything. Lucy was there when Ava's underwear was covered in blood for the very first time. Lucy was there to teach Ava how to look as unappealing as possible during visitor days at the home. Lucy was even there when Ava's face was beaten so badly that she had to be spoon-fed applesauce for a straight week. Turns out, Sister Marie had a formidable backhand. Ava lost count of the number of girls who attempted to run away, only to come back a few days later with tall tales to tell of their humbling experiences 'in the streets'. Ava was convinced that sticking it out inside the yellow-tinted tree house was far better than roughing it during the brutal East Coast winters. But Ava made a plan and she diligently stuck to the plan. There wasn't one day within those four walls that she didn't scheme and dream away. London. The day she turned eighteen, she would be wheels up to London. It's a place she'd heard her mother talk about countless times. A place she was confident encapsulated her mother's bright spirit. A place she would draw like an etch a sketch each day in her mind, only to be shaken clean to start brand new the next day. She would scratch and claw all the way to London if she had to. And, turns out, that's exactly what she had to do.

That first month in London was one of the darkest seasons in Ava's life. While she was not oblivious to the fact that London was far from affordable, she didn't expect the extremes she would have to go through to make ends meet. Ava couldn't exactly complain about cleaning toilets when she was quite literally penniless. But Ava chipped away at it. After a year in London, she built up enough credit to pay the application fee and half of the first-semester fee for King's College. It was there that she met a professor who steered her to the Architecture School of Design, and it was also there that she mastered the course on 'How to accrue a hefty debt 101'. During her internship, she met a gentle yet somewhat handsy lead Architect whose stay-at-home wife needed help with her kids. When Ava wasn't working, she was shepherding two bratty twins around from one posh recreational center to another. It was during this time that she serendipitously stumbled upon Max Greenfield in an ultra-modern coffee shop just on the outskirts of Kensington. And it was there that Ava's life rerouted. There would be no more switchbacks, just straightaways. Straightaways into Max Greenfield's heart and the nice safety net that came along with it.

Ava picks up speed. If she can reach a certain mile per hour, maybe, just maybe, she can quiet the chatter in her mind. She takes a sharp right turn down the long gravel road that leads to Brophy's parking lot. It's a bit foggy, so it's tough for Ava to determine if it's the right road. She pauses, trying to gather her bearings. She's always been terrible with directions, and this is no exception.

Ava whips her head around with just enough time to see a white Chevy pickup truck barreling down the gravel drive. It's coming straight for her and showing no signs of stopping.

Ava jumps into the ditch on the side of the road. She's on her hands and knees as the white truck accelerates past her. She squints, trying to get a clear view of the license plate.

Did she imagine this? It is early. Maybe she is still in a sleep haze.

No. She definitely saw the truck.

She's lucky she didn't have any headphones in. Ava's never been able to run with headphones. For her, running is about clearing her mind of all the incessant chatter. She refuses to run with Max because he turns the volume all the way up on his headphones so she can hear it as he runs next to her. That, combined with his heavy breathing, is enough to send her into a tailspin.

Ava looks around to see if anyone else is around to bear witness to this near accident. Of course, she's alone. Who would be up at five in the morning in this town?

Ava brushes off the gravel that is stuck to her knees.

She's hit with yet another vivid flashback of when she was ten years old at Sister Catherine's. Ava is surrounded by a group of girls who are yelling at her. One of the girls pushes Ava to the ground and spits on her head. The other girls laugh and saunter away. Lucy offers her hand to Ava and helps her onto her feet. Ava brushes off the dirt from her knees. "Stick with me, kid. I'll protect you."

Lucy says.

Ava is brought back to the present as her phone is ringing with Max's name on the screen. She screens his call. She does not have time to talk to him right now. Not after she almost got run over at five in the morning.

Where the hell did that truck go? Ava is looking in every possible direction but finds no trace of the car. It's probably a junkie townie who is just getting off an all-night bender and is high off their ass.

Right, that's most likely it, Ava thinks. She needs to remember where she is. She's not in Kensington anymore. This would never happen in Kensington.

If it were up to Max, he would have wanted to stay in his posh highrise in downtown London. Ava begged and pleaded until she finally got him to agree to move to the suburbs. Ava knows Max misses the downtown hustle and bustle, but Kensington is where they need to be for appearance's sake. She knows Max knows that, too. Ava's not really one for keeping up with appearances but she knows what she signed up for by marrying Max. Max's parents were clear on that. If a no-name swain were to marry their son, she must know the rules. There would be no free handouts (their words, not hers). So, Ava has done her best to keep their prestigious social calendar booked and busy. In reality, it's Max who puts up a fight whenever they have to attend yet another gala or fundraiser. He doesn't buy into all the hoity-toity bullshit. It's what initially attracted Ava to Max. He is authentically himself. Take it or leave it. Nowadays, Ava has to bribe Max to change into his black tie suit when he throws a tantrum like a child. His radical authenticity seems to have lost its charm over the years. She knows Max feels the same. His comments about how much Ava has changed seem to be more frequent these days. When Ava first met Max, she was less than impressed by the prominent family Max comes from. Where other girls may have felt starstruck,

Ava merely felt ambivalent. Max loved that about Ava. She

was driven by her own success. She could care less about

how much money Max had. Ava made a promise to herself

at a young age that she would make it on her own. She

wouldn't depend on anyone. And while marriage changed

that promise a bit, she still has kept true to her word. It's

rare for Ava to dip into their shared bank account. For the

most part, the money she earns is the money she spends.

Ava resumes her jogging pace until she's at her

rental car. She climbs up into the SUV and steers the

vehicle in the direction of Happy Hollow Road. She

decided last night before she went to bed that she would

give one last go at talking to that wire-haired squatter. She

really does not want to get lawyers involved. That, in fact,

is the very last thing she needs.

Before she forgets, she dials Max on the Bluetooth.

He should be in the middle of his morning by now and

probably just on his way to work. That's the beauty of working for your Dad's big wig company: you get to choose your own hours. Max would never understand the lengths and hurdles Ava has had to go through to get to where she is today, which is precisely why she's never fully opened up to him about her past. When they first started dating, she used to lie about where she lived. Every time Max would drop her off and ask to come in, she claimed she had a crazy roommate who didn't want any visitors whatsoever. Plus, Max had a penthouse suite right next to her office. It couldn't have been any easier. Convenience was the key to Ava securing a literal key to his place. This eventually lead to Ava moving in less than six months after dating.

Max immediately picks up.

"Ava, what the hell?"

"I know, I know, Max. I'm sorry. Trust me, I can explain. Yesterday was a day… to say the least."

"Are you okay? I was beyond worried about you."

"I'm so sorry, Max. I wish I could have called you sooner. It seems like there is an issue with the will." Ava hangs a right onto Happy Hollow Road.

"An issue? What kind of issue?" Max genuinely sounds concerned.

"My parent's house has a squatter who refuses to vacate the property."

"A squatter?"

Ava is at the gates of the property. She notices a Toyota Highlander that seems to have clipped one of the large oak trees planted next to the garage. Ava remembers the roots of that tree stubbing her toe one morning when she was young. It was a bloodbath. She thought her toe was going to fall off. It's crazy how all it took was one visit to this property for all these memories to come back to her.

"Hello? Ava!" Max is irritated now.

How quickly he can shift, Ava thinks.

"Yes, sorry. A squatter. It's okay. It's being handled. I hope to wrap things up today and be on the first flight out of here tomorrow morning." Ava does not take her eyes off the Toyota Highlander. The door to the Highlander seems to be halfway open. She can't quite make out who is inside of the car.

"Ava. I'm worried about you. Do you need me to fly over there?"

"Oh gosh, absolutely not Max. Thank you, but I promise you I have it handled, my love."

"It doesn't really sound like that's the case, babe."

Ava is irritated now. If there's one thing she can't stand, it's being undermined. "Max, please. Just let me handle this, ok? I'm more than capable of handling this. I have to go but I will call you soon. Bye!"

Ava clicks off the phone before Max has time to ask additional questions. She definitely does not have time for the legendary Max Greenfield inquisition.

Ava parks the SUV and hustles out of the car and through the gates.

"Hello! Hello, are you okay?" she shouts.

Ava is standing right inside the gates, waiting for an answer. When no answer comes, she inches closer and closer to the car.

Once she's a few feet away from the car, she peeks her head inside to see who is sitting in the driver's seat.

It's the wirey-haired squatter. The left front of her car is dented in. The tree definitely did some damage. Ava hustles to the car and works to force open the door a bit more. She can't just leave her here, can she? No. Clearly, she needs Ava's help.

"Hello? Are you okay? Do you need help?" Ava asks.

The squatter lets out a few inaudible moans.

She's alive. Thank God.

The smell of whiskey hits Ava's nostrils. She's drunk. It's not even noon, and she's as drunk as a skunk.

The squatter has a little gash above her left eye that is steadily pouring out blood. Ava gags. She's never been good around blood.

Ava puts her arm under the squatter's shoulder and lifts her out of the car. Thank goodness she weighs all of ninety-five pounds. Ava is lean but strong. Pilates five days a week will do that to you. It's like a religion for Ava.

"Ooof. There you go. Easy now. Can you walk?"

"Yeshhh. God dawmn itttt." The blonde says, slurring her words.

Ava leans her up against the car. She steadies herself before slowly leading her across the driveway and up the three rickety steps of the house.

They are barely inside the house when Ava gets hit with another flashback. It's like she couldn't stop the flashbacks if she tried. Being in this house and on this property is enough to make it feel like she was living here just yesterday.

This time, she's at the top of the staircase, hiding behind a wall so her parents can't see. Her parents are engaged in a screaming match.

Her mother screams, "You're a fucking liar! I know you're lying to me. Just tell me the truth!"

"You want the truth! You're a crazy bitch who's lost her goddamn mind!" Her father screams back.

Ava's mother grabs the car keys and heads for the door.

"I'm going to get to the bottom of this. Trust me when I say I will find out. I will not stop until I find out."

Without another word, Ava's mother slams the door so hard that the hinges on the door frame shift to the right.

"Ahhhhhh," The squatter moans.

Ava is brought back to reality. They are walking through the long hallway to the family room with the million-dollar view. This is where all of their family gatherings would be and where Ava would spend virtually every waking moment.

Ava eases the squatter down onto the couch and scans the room. It's a shithole. Trash is scattered everywhere. Junk covers every corner of the room. It's still the same key lime green color as it was all those years ago. Ava's mom hated that color. She begged her dad to paint it another color, but her dad was stubborn and wanted to keep it as is. Call it an old-school mentality, but Ava's dad always got his way. He ruled the roost, so to speak.

Ava picks up the squatter's head to try to wake her up. She flicks her cheek with her finger.

"Hey! Hey, wake up. Where do you keep the emergency kit? Huh?"

The blonde slumps back down on the couch and falls instantly into a deep sleep.

C'mon, Ava thinks to herself. Did she really think this fool would have an emergency kit? She doesn't even have a proper trash bin.

Just as she's about to start rummaging through the kitchen in search of a makeshift bandaid, the squatter's phone rings. Ava hustles back to the couch and grabs the phone from the squatter's pocket.

She answers on the third ring, "Hello?"

"Tessa, where the hell are you? I've been sitting here for forty minutes waiting on you." A male with a deep voice is speaking back over the other end of the phone.

"Oh, um. Hi, this isn't Tessa. This is..." Ava realizes how stupid she sounds, "I'm with Tessa now. She seemed to have hit a tree at the house, and I helped her inside. She's okay but definitely a little banged up."

"I'll be right there."

"Wait!"

Before Ava can finish her sentence, the line clicks off. She forgot to ask the male who he was. Maybe this is a good thing, Ava thinks. Maybe he's somehow tied to Tessa, and she can discuss the will with him and finally get her to leave the property.

Yes, this is a good turn of events. Ava wills this to be true.

It's about fifteen minutes before a car comes blazing through the iron gates.

Ava is peeking out from behind a curtain. A tall man with shaggy blonde hair exits the car. He's wearing worn-out jeans and a tight V-neck t-shirt. Too tight for guys to be wearing, Ava thinks. Although, she can't argue that his muscles flexing underneath that paper-thin piece of fabric are nice eye candy.

Without knocking, he barges through the front door and looks Ava up and down.

"Where is she?" he asks.

Ava points to the living room. Without another word, he beelines it down the long hallway and shakes the blonde awake.

"Ahhh. Leave me alone!" the blonde manages to blurt out.

"Jesus Tessa. It's not even noon! You promised me!" The male is pacing back and forth as the morning sun starts to fill the living room. That was always Ava's favorite part of this room. At the right time of day, the sun would reflect off the water, and the entire room would feel like you were in a giant fish tank.

The guy turns his attention to Ava.

"Who the hell are you? You one of her junkie friends who got her twisted this way?"

"No… No, I'm…" Ava stumbles over her words. "I'm Ava Greenfield. My parents owned this house." Ava looks around the room, still trying to understand it all herself. "I own this house. I'm on the will." Ava fishes in her purse for the will and hands over the papers to him.

"Tessa seems to think she has the right to live here," Ava continues, "She told my lawyer she has legal documents to prove she is lawfully a resident here."

He scans the papers and hands them back to Ava. "Christ. Today is clearly not my day."

He heads into the kitchen. There is a half wall that separates the kitchen from the living room so Ava can still see the top portion of his body. Ava remembers when her dad used to use that wall to pretend like he was going down a flight of stairs. Ava would be in a ball of laughter on the floor every time.

"What are you doing?" Ava asks.

"You want some coffee?"

Ava realizes this is the longest she's gone without coffee in the morning. She usually has three cups before getting ready to start her commute to the downtown office. The itch has now become an obvious scratch.

"I would love some," Ava says. "Thank you."

An awkward two minutes pass by while they both wait for the K-Cups to brew the coffee.

He grabs the two mugs of coffee and motions for Ava to join him on the back deck. The entire right side of the deck is weathered and worn from the saltwater air. Ava is careful about where she places her feet, making sure to avoid the termite-ridden floorboards.

He hands Ava her coffee, "Shoot, I should have asked if you liked creamer. Although, I would be surprised if there's anything besides booze in that fridge."

"That's okay. I like it black." Ava remarks almost too confidently. She tyring not to sound like a psychopath.

Another silent minute passes as they both stare out into the vastness of the Chesapeake Bay.

"So, who are you?"

"Who am I?" the male asks.

"Yeah. I mean, how do you know Tessa?" Ava motions inside to Tessa, who is still passed out on the couch.

"Ah. She's my sister. Well, my adopted sister but my sister nonetheless. I'm Tommy." He extends his hand. Ava takes it awkwardly. "I'm sorry about coming at you like that in there. I'm just very protective of Tessa. She always has losers lurking around, and I just assumed –"

"Don't worry about it," Ava waves him off.

What a shame, Ava thinks. As much as she dislikes her squatter, she never wants to see someone as down and out as Tessa. It feels weird to even call her Tessa. She knows virtually nothing about this woman.

"I should have called right away. I just didn't know what to do other than get her inside." Ava blurts out

"You did the right thing. Thank you." Tommy says "I wish I could say this is the first time this has happened, but it seems these relapses are becoming ever more frequent."

"Relapses?" Ava asks.

"I was waiting for her outside her AA meeting when I called. Once she was a no-show, I knew something was up." Tommy faces Ava so he's looking at her right in the eyes. "She wasn't even sober for a week this time."

"Wow. I'm so sorry." Ava says, this time really meaning it.

Tommy turns back to face the bay, "So what's this all about the will?"

Ava is brought back to the reality of why she's here—standing on this rickety deck that looks like it may collapse at any moment—talking to this strange yet attractive man who seems to be making her sweat a bit too much.

"I received a call from Thompkins Bay Law Firm. They told me they had found my parent's will. My parents died when I was seven, so you can imagine my shock."

"Shit."

"Yeah. Shit." Ava echoes.

Tommy motions to the overgrown lawn that backs up to the bay, "So you lived here? You grew up in this house?"

"I did," Ava says. She motions to the dock way out in the distance. The dock is now halfway underwater, barely visible. "See that dock there? I used to set oyster traps every morning with my dad. I can still smell the brine on my hands to this day."

"I own an oyster farm." Tommy holds up his hands and smells his right hand. "I'm starting to think it's my natural pheromones now."

Of course he's an oyster farmer, Ava thinks. What are the bloody odds?

"So your sister, Tessa…Does she have another place to stay?" Ava selfishly asks. She's slowly nudging the conversation in the direction she wants it to go. "If she needs help, I can put her up in a hotel or an Airbnb for a few weeks."

"An AirBnB!?" Tommy laughs. "This town definitely does not have an Airbnb."

Right. How stupid of Ava to suggest that.

"I'm staying at the DoubleTree in town. It's actually quite lovely – you know, all things considered."

There she goes again. shitting on this town any second she gets. It's not like she's purposely doing it. The words almost flow from her subconscious mind before she has any control to stop them.

"Tessa is a fighter. She won't go down without swinging, I'll tell you that."

Great, just her luck, Ava thinks.

"I really would like to settle this without going to court. I think it's the best move for both parties to avoid that."

Tommy looks back inside at Tessa. She's awake now and running her hands through her wild hair. Tommy's eyes soften.

"I'll talk to her. See if I can get through to her. No promises, though."

"Of course. Thank you. I would really appreciate that."

Ava turns to head back inside. She is so beyond ready to get the hell out of this place. It feels as if her throat is slowly closing in with each passing minute she's on this property.

"What are you doing tonight?" Tommy asks before she can get inside.

"Excuse me?" Ava asks. She spins back around to face Tommy.

"I wanted to invite you to my oyster farm."

"Oh. Thank you, but I was planning on being wheels-up back to London early tomorrow."

Tommy steps closer, closing in on the gap between the two of them. It's an awkward distance, not close enough to be touching but not far enough away to give Ava any kind of personal space.

"Look, you want me to speak with her, right?"

Ava nods slowly, mainly because she's not sure what she wants right now.

"The only way I'm going to get through to her is if she's dead sober. That will take at least two days, considering today will be a wash as she shakes off her hangover." Tommy steps another inch closer to Ava. They are centimeters away from touching. "Might as well check out the farm while we kill some time."

Ava doesn't have two more days. Two more days would mean two more days of not being completely dialed into her project at work. Two more days would mean two more days apart from Max. Two more days would mean forty-eight more hours in this godforsaken place. Saying no should be the obvious and only answer here.

"Okay. Sure." Ava replies, almost immediately. She has no idea where that response came from. Everything in her body is begging for her to get out of this town. Why is she agreeing to two more days here? Why is this man standing so damn close to her? Why is she feeling the slightest hint of desire brewing inside of her?

"Great. I'll meet you at Chessie's Market Marina at five tonight."

"Isn't the best time to oyster early in the morning before sunrise?" Ava asks.

"Yes, but that would mean you would miss the iconic Chesapeake sunset," Tommy says.

If Ava's being honest, she's always preferred sunrises to sunsets. The Chesapeake Bay sunrise has always held a firm grasp on her heart. She remembers a time when she was out setting traps with her dad. Little Ava is dressed in a sweatshirt, shivering as she sits shotgun on her dad's beat-up Boston Whaler. It's four-thirty in the morning and the entire world is eerily still.

"And drop," her dad instructs.

Ava drops a large oyster trap into the bay, following his instructions perfectly. As her dad meanders into the mouth of the channel, the Whaler comes to a slow. A large cargo like ship is sitting less than a quarter of a mile away. It's too dark and foggy on the water to really make out the features of the ship.

"Dad, what is that? Where are their lights?" little Ava asks.

"Shhhh. Don't worry. They're just lost." Ava's dad replies. He grabs his flashlight and starts blinking the flashlight on and off for about twenty seconds.

Ava looks at her dad with confusion. Her dad pats her on the top of her head.

"There there, Ako. I was just helping them find their way back home. Hold on."

Her dad punches it on the accelerator, and the Whaler makes a wide U-turn, heading back into the narrow channel. Ava glances back one last time at the mysterious boat, not knowing why a lump suddenly worked itself up into her throat.

"You ok?" Tommy asks, bringing Ava back to the present. His hand has made its way onto the small of her back.

Ava's hand remains unmoved on the door knob.

"Yeah, sorry," Ava says, turning the doorknob, "Thank you again for your help. See you tonight."

Ava steps back inside and wills herself to walk as fast as possible down the long hallway and out the front door. Her front door.

––––––––––––

TESSA

Tessa's in the middle of a dream—one that's visited her a few other times. She's three years old, swinging on a swing at the playground. A tall man with a blue baseball cap grabs her feet and stops her abruptly mid-swing. He bends down and tucks a piece of her blonde hair behind her ear.

"You look just like her, you know," he says.

She looks up at the man but can't seem to make out his face or any of his features. And then he's gone, almost like a ghost. He disappears into the thick fog of the morning. That's where her dream ends. That's where it frustratingly always ends.

"I'm awake. I'm awake, for fucks sake!" Tessa groans as Tommy shakes her.

He hands her a glass of lukewarm water, "Drink this. All of it."

Tessa knows better than to refute Tommy when he's like this. She gulps down the water.

"I bought you two days."

"Two days?" Tessa asks as she sits up a bit straighter.

"Two days for you to pack up your things and get out of here. When were you gonna tell me?"

"Tell you what?"

"That you don't live here. Legally, I mean."

Tessa stands up and steadies herself. She's wobbly and groggy from sleeping all morning. "What are you talking about? I live here."

"Why is that woman claiming she rightfully owns this property? She showed me the will to prove it."

"I have no idea why she's claiming that. You should really read the fine print. People can fake anything nowadays."

"Tessa. How did you get access to this house?" Tommy presses, ignoring her smug comment.

"Jesus, Tommy. You make it sound like I'm some sort of criminal."

Tommy lets out a tired sigh, "Tessa, please. Just tell me."

Tessa rolls her eyes, "Fine. Since you want to be all nosy. A woman I met in AA told me about this property that her family owned. She offered me the place to stay when Mom and Dad kicked me out. And when you kicked me out." She looks right at Tommy when she says that last sentence, "It was a really good price that I couldn't pass up."

Tommy starts pacing back and forth in the living room again.

"It's legit, Tommy. I signed a contract and everything."

"Well, where is it?"

Tessa looks at Tommy with those puppy dog eyes. It's how she's been able to get away with things for most of her life. Just one look usually magically transforms people into putty. It's her superpower. A superpower that seems to have lost its magic on her parents and Tommy.

"The contract, Tessa!" Tommy yells.

"I have to find it! It's around here somewhere. You don't need to yell!"

"And if you can't find it?"

"I'll stay with you, duh." Tessa jokes.

Tommy gives her a look that warns her to tread lightly. Tessa's almost positive she's the reason why Tommy's last relationship imploded. Tessa stayed with

Tommy and his girlfriend for a few weeks after her parents

kicked her out. Tommy's girlfriend resented Tessa the

minute she walked through the door. Eventually, the

girlfriend gave Tommy an ultimatum: Tessa or her. Clearly,

she didn't know Tommy that well. He would never go

against Tessa. Especially when she was at her lowest point.

There have been a lot of low points throughout Tessa's

twenty-seven years, but this particular time felt different.

Tessa blew past rock bottom and dug herself so deep not

even the undertaker could save her. She was just off the

heels of a two-day bender and headed home to sleep it off

when a local cop tried to pull her over for rolling through a

stop sign. Instead of stopping, though, Tessa decided to up

the ante and start a full-on car chase. A car chase that ended

in Tessa running into an empty school bus. The entire

debacle made the local news. Tessa's parents were

mortified and spent almost all of their retirement savings

bailing her out of jail. Because Tessa's dad was friendly

with the Chestertown Chief of Police, he was able to get her charges reduced to two counts of driving under the influence so she would avoid any serious jail time. Tessa's license was revoked for two years, and she was required to attend AA for those two years. Tessa's parents kicked her out, so Tommy had no choice but to take her in. Eventually, the girlfriend moved out and Tessa thought it would be just her and Tommy again, like the good old days. However, Tommy seemed to have also hit his wits end with Tessa and gave her three weeks to find her own place. Those two years seem like forever ago. While Tessa's not exactly sober by any means, she has significantly cleaned up her act to avoid any further legal trouble. That's a win in Tessa's book.

"If I can't find it, I'll just ask my landlord for another copy of the lease. Ok?" Tessa says.

"Sure Tessy. Ok." Tommy does not have the energy to fight with Tessa. He's choosing to let it go – for now.

"What's this I hear about some coffee?" Tessa says as Tommy's already halfway out the door and showing no signs of turning back.

———————

LUCY

Why is she back at this house? Why doesn't she just go back to London already? And who is this man she's talking to?

Lucy is crouched behind a thick row of bramblewood bushes. She's looking through a pair of rusted red binoculars that are pointed directly at Ava standing on the back deck. She and the man are engaged in a conversation, and judging by their body language, it looks serious.

The man looks over in Lucy's direction.

She drops the binoculars and ducks her head.

There's no way he could have seen her, Lucy reminds herself. She shutters. Just being back on this property gives her chills. Being back here is not good.

She picks back up the binoculars.

The man now has his hand on the lower part of Ava's back.

Lucy pulls her phone out of her pocket and zooms in so the man and Ava are in clear view. She snaps a picture right before Ava heads back inside.

————————

AVA

Ava is signing a stack of papers that sit in front of her on Sam Thompkins's desk. Sam watches her with uneasiness.

"And you're sure you want to do this?" Sam asks.

Ava nods as she places down his fancy ballpoint pen.

"I'm sure. I talked to my husband this morning. If this will result in this whole thing being over and done with, it's what we need to do. She needs money. That was clear during my visit yesterday." Ava scoffs.

It was actually Max who suggested offering Tessa the money as a bribe for her to vacate the property. He still doesn't understand why Ava is even pursuing this, given they don't really need the money. She's lived decades without this property. Why is it so important to her now, he asked. In reality, this has never been about the money. This is about righting a wrong. In a way, it's about salvaging a childhood that was stripped from Ava all too soon. Max will never understand, but that's okay. He doesn't need to understand it. He has no dog in this fight, Ava thinks.

Sam nods, "Right, well… let me get to it. I'll work on drafting everything and getting it sent out by the end of the day today."

"Please, as fast as you can. I'm sure you understand my need to return to my work and family in London."

"Of course," Sam says.

Ava is sitting in her rental car and glances down at her trembling hands. She knows she should start the car and make the right turn that leads down the road back to her hotel. So why can't she start the car?

She finally turns on the ignition. She makes a sharp left towards Chessie's Market Marina.

Everything in Ava's logical brain is telling her to turn around. She's not yet on the boat. She still has time. She can call it a brief lapse of judgment if she just turns around now.

She pushes out the string of logical thoughts pulsating through her brain as she parks the car and walks down the dock toward Tommy's boat. Tommy grabs her hand as he helps her into his Boston Whaler. Ironically, it's

a similar make and model to the Whaler her dad used to
have all those years ago.

Tommy hands Ava a grey sweatshirt with a UNC
logo in baby blue letters written across the chest.

"Here, it's gonna get cold out there. Especially once
we get going."

Ava graciously accepts the gesture. "You went to
UNC?"

"I did. Studied marine biology. I originally wanted
to be a deep-sea diver. I wanted to travel the world
restoring our coral reefs." Tommy laughs, but it's a
somewhat forceful and pained laugh.

Ava can't help but note that they both care about the
planet. It's refreshing to find a guy who actually cares
about someone or something other than himself. Max uses
so many plastic water bottles that he could fill this entire
Whaler with them. Ava has tried to lecture him about the
consequences he is causing for the future generation, but

Max seems to think the future generation can fight their own battles.

Ava pulls the sweatshirt over her head. Max's cologne is still lingering on his sweatshirt, making Ava feel some kind of way. It smells like the perfect mixture of sandpaper mixed with whiskey.

"What happened?" Ava asks.

"My dad got diagnosed with Parkinson's and he needed someone to take over the farm."

"So you stepped up?"

"So I stepped up," Tommy confirms. His voice trails off as he focuses on navigating the boat out of the marina.

"Do you like it? I mean, you must like it if you're still doing it."

"I like being out on the water. This body of water is my second home. It's all I've ever known." Tommy turns to look at Ava to add extra emphasis, "I believe the universe places you in situations you're meant to be in. It brings you to people you are meant to meet."

Ava blushes.

"Hang on tight."

"Wha–" Before Ava can finish that sentence, the Whaler kicks it into high gear. Ava grabs ahold of the seat in front of her with one hand as she tries to wrangle her hair with the other.

The cold gust of air shocks her system, but after a few minutes, it feels nice—almost freeing. Ava needed this. She needed a good shock to the system after these past few days.

The Whaler is starting to slow as it pulls into a narrow and windy channel that dumps you into a U-shaped estuary.

"It's breathtaking," Ava comments, more to herself than anyone.

Tommy picks up the anchor and his back muscles strain as he tosses it overboard. She needs to stop staring, but she can't quite seem to take her eyes off of him. What in the world has gotten into her?

"We call it the Lucky Shoe because of the horseshoe shape."

"It's the first thing I noticed," Ava admits.

Tommy hands her a pair of waders, "You're gonna need these. Apologies, they may be a little big. They're my dad's old pair."

"Does your dad still come out here?" Ava asks as she slips into the oversized waders.

"He did, but closer to the end, he didn't want to leave the house. Parkinson's took both his body and his personality. He was a shell of a human towards the end. I kept picturing we'd take one last boat ride to this place and have this beautiful moment between the two of us where we would say our final goodbye. But – well, that never ended up happening. He was gone quicker than we all expected."

"I'm so sorry." Ava's never been good about talking about death. She much prefers to skirt right around the subject and move on to greener and happier pastures.

"Let me show you around," Tommy says as he extends his hand.

She takes Tommy's hand and exits the Whaler carefully. She's always been a clutz, and she would be absolutely mortified if she tripped and fell face-first into the water. Once she's steady on her two feet, she follows Tommy as he wades in the water towards the oyster traps. There are rows and rows of oyster traps, all strategically placed based on the tide schedules.

Ava remembers studying the tide schedules with her dad in his home office. He would quiz her each morning. The more accurate prediction of the tide time, the more minutes Ava got to drive the boat while sitting on her dad's lap.

Tommy picks up one of the traps and shakes it.

"Few little guys in there." He puts the trap back in the water. "You'd be shocked at what people will pay for the little guys. Sometimes the little ones are the best sellers."

"Why do you think that is?" Ava asks.

"I have no idea. I guess people like to root for the underdog."

Ava laughs because his remark is all too relatable. She's been the underdog for most of her life. It wasn't until after she married Max that she finally felt that she 'made it'. Although, if she's being honest, she's always felt a sense of imposter syndrome. That feeling never seems to go away, especially when you're used to being the underdog for so long.

Tommy continues walking until he pauses at a lone trap that isn't connected to the other traps. It seems almost on an island, all by itself.

"What's this?" Ava asks curiously.

"This here is what Lucky Shoe is all about," Tommy smirks.

He pulls out the trap and opens the tiny trap door. He picks up one of the mishappen oysters and hands it to Ava.

Ava runs her fingers over the oyster's ridged shell.

"It's called an Akoya oyster."

Ava goes numb. She's pretty sure her heart stopped beating. Did Tommy really just say what she think he said?

"They're one of the rarest oysters to find because of what's inside. Inside is one of the purest cultured pearls you'll probably ever lay eyes on." Tommy says as he whips out a tiny yellow oyster knife from his back pocket. He gets a firm grip on the oyster and jabs the knife halfway through the top of the oyster. He shimmies the knife a few times before the oyster finally breaks open in two.

A single tear traces down Ava's nose. Another tear trickles down her cheek. After all these years of keeping the floodgates at bay, the tears finally come. Right here at Lucky Shoe farm, of all places. More tears are begging to be set free. Ava wipes them away before Tommy notices.

Tommy continues, oblivious to Ava's change in demeanor, "It's a shame because they used to be everywhere and anywhere in the Chesapeake. But then – well, then people got greedy. The locals started looting the Chesapeake for all the Akoya oysters they could get their hands on. They turned a nice profit. People paid top dollar for these pearls. They eventually became endangered, but I still have a secret spot where you can find them. You really have to look, but they're there. They've always been there."

Tommy looks Ava dead in the eyes as he says this last sentence.

"Why do you keep them in here? Why don't you sell them?" Ava asks, trying to ignore the fire in her belly that seems to be slowly churning.

Tommy blushes, "You're going to think I'm crazy."

"No I won't. Tell me."

"I'm kind of saving them."

"Saving them for what?"

Tommy runs his tan hands through his unruly blonde hair. "I want to give them to my future wife – or if I have a daughter, I want to give them to her one day. I have more than enough to make a necklace or bracelet."

Ava's heart flip-flops. Is this really happening? Ava goes to reach for her own pearl necklace that sits on her collarbone. She can't quite grasp it underneath the thick sweatshirt. After Ava's dad gave her the Akoyo pearl, Ava kept that pearl in a safe place only she would know about. Just after she moved to London, she went to the most expensive jewelry store she could find and had them transform the pearl into a necklace. Since that day, she has never taken that necklace off. It's a part of her now, both literally and figuratively.

"I –I…" Ava stutters, "I have a pearl necklace."

"I noticed. It's the first thing I noticed about you, actually."

Ava can't breathe. It feels like an elephant has sat on her chest. It's the first thing he noticed? Max has never once asked Ava about her pearl necklace. He either does not notice it or does not care. Either way, having Tommy standing here telling her he noticed something so very intimate about her is sending her heart and mind into a nosedive.

Before Ava can even process what is happening, she grabs Tommy and pulls him into her. Her lips are on his before either of them can object to it. Tommy is caught off guard at first, but he quickly leans just as passionately into Ava until they are fully intertwined together.

Tommy's hands are through Ava's hair as she sucks on his bottom lip. It tastes like peppermint and salt brine. It's the sexiest combination Ava has ever tasted. Tommy is grabbing Ava's hips as Ava opens her mouth wider. She's moaning for more.

Tommy reaches his hand to touch one of Ava's breasts.

Ava suddenly pushes him off of her. It's like a light switched on inside of Ava. A light that illuminated the very real consequence of her actions.

Tommy looks confused by this sudden change of pace.

Ava wipes the saliva from her lip, "No. I'm sorry. I can't. I'm married."

"I know. I can see the ring."

"This isn't me. I– I don't know what came over me. I'm sorry, I shouldn't have done that."

"I'm not mad about it."

"I need to go home. Can you please take me back to the marina?"

"Ava —"

"Please," Ava pleads. Her voice is sharp and foreign. It's a voice she only reserves for work meetings and it feels very out of place being used here in this estuary. Her deep ocean-blue eyes have grown serious.

Tommy lowers his eyes and nods his head. They both head back to the Whaler that is bobbing carefree with the tide.

Tommy offers his hand to help Ava back into the boat, but this time, she climbs aboard without his help. It's an unspoken gesture that speaks volumes.

The entire boat ride back is eerily quiet. Neither Ava nor Tommy say a single word. It's getting dark, and Tommy turns on the boat lights as they approach the desolate marina. The lights shine on the profile of Tommy's face. He looks like a hurt puppy. That look is killing Ava.

She looks away. She can't afford to be weak right now. What she just did was out of character and she will surely be reeling from the implications of her actions for some time. How could she be so careless? This place has a dark cloud that always seems to be following her around. How silly of her to think that after all these years and after all that distance, this time would be any different.

Tommy eases the boat into its slip with an experts touch. Ava hops off the boat just as Tommy is killing the ignition.

She looks down at Tommy, "I'm sorry. I'm not that girl." Ava is now crying and shaking her head, "I'm not that girl." She's letting the tears fall fast and heavy. Ava was convinced her body had lost the ability to cry. But here she is now with her tear-soaked face, remembering how to cry. Remembering how good it feels to let it all out.

Before Tommy can say anything back, Ava turns and runs down the dock toward the marina parking lot.

Without even thinking, she runs past her car and the parking lot. She's doing what she always does when the pain starts creeping in: she runs. If she can just run fast enough, maybe the demons won't be able to catch her.

She's running back to the hotel in her dress and sandals. She still has on Tommy's UNC sweatshirt.

Just as she makes a right onto High Street, she hears a car honking it's horn from behind her.

Shit, she thinks. Ava turns around. Of course. It's Lucy.

Ava has a few seconds to pull herself together. She wipes the tears from her eyes and tries to put on a smile. Mascara is streaked down her cheeks, making it obvious Ava is anything but fine.

Lucy pulls the car over and rolls down the window.

"Ava? Are you ok?"

Ava lets out a frantic laugh, "Oh yeah, I'm fine! I just got a bit turned around. I'm on my way back to the hotel."

"Hop in. I'll drive you back," Lucy says.

"Oh no! Thank you, but seriously, I'm okay."

"Well, for starters, you're headed in the wrong direction. The hotel is about three miles the other way."

Ava sighs. She's left with no choice but to open Lucy's passenger car door and hop in. Her poor sense of direction has failed her, yet again.

As soon as Ava buckles her seatbelt, Lucy turns her whole body to face her. She looks concerned. "Ava, are you really okay?"

Ava lets that question hang in the air for longer than she should. Is she really okay? What does okay even mean to her anymore? Has she ever really been okay?

Finally, as if the finale crescendo in a musical, Ava comes crashing down in Lucy's Honda. She lets out twenty-five years of pent-up emotion. Twenty-five years of running from the very thing that made her. Twenty-five years of escapism. Twenty-five years of loneliness. Twenty-five years of wishing for anything but here. And yet, it feels so good to get it all out. To finally come undone. To finally let her pristine image she worked so hard to polish crack wide open.

Lucy lets Ava release it all. She does nothing but hold her hand as Ava peels back all the layers. After a good five minutes, Ava says something that makes the hair on Lucy's arm stand tall.

"I never thanked you for that night." Ava says through sniffles, " I wanted to thank you. For saving my life."

LUCY

I'd been wracking my brain on ways I could run

into her again. To see what other tidbits of information I could get from her. I mainly wanted to know when she was going to leave this town for good. She's already been here too long. It's time for her to go. And here she is, looking like a damn fool on the side of the road, wearing a ridiculously oversized sweatshirt that obviously belongs to a guy. The kicker is her mascara-soaked eyes. She's clearly in a fragile place, and this is the exact opportunity I needed. This is my in. But all I can think about right now is what Ava just said to me—thanking me. So she remembers that night? I had always hoped Ava had pushed that night out of her consciousness. I'd hoped she locked the key and threw it the fuck away. Of course she didn't. She is her father's daughter, after all. She's going to mess it all up. I can't let that happen. I won't let that happen.

Lucy's car is parked outside the hotel, but neither Lucy nor Ava makes any move to exit the car.

Ava is telling Lucy everything—her fertility troubles, her imposter syndrome in London, a marriage that is anything but sunflowers, and, most importantly, the squatter. She even divulged the details of her make-out session with Tommy on the oyster farm just a few hours ago.

"I mean, what am I doing? He's a stranger, for heaven's sake!" Ava says, "I mean, I kissed him! And the truth is, I kind of liked it. What does that even mean?"

She's looking at Lucy with desperation in her eyes. She's looking for an answer to this madness that has just descended upon her. She's looking for a rope, for a way out. Lucy seems to be out of rope this time.

"It can mean whatever you want it to mean," Lucy says. "You don't need to assign a label to it. It sounds like a fleeting moment where your emotions got the best of you. It happens to us all."

"But what about Max!?" Ava asks.

"He doesn't have to know if you don't want him to know."

"How can I not tell Max?"

Lucy looks Ava square in the eyes, "If you want to keep a secret, you must also be able to hide it from yourself."

Ava stiffens. She's frozen in fear. Fear of the past. Fear of the future. Most of all, fear that Lucy isn't just referring to Max now. Something much deeper is attached to that last sentence she spoke.

Ava's phone starts to buzz. She reaches into her pocket and looks at the screen, expecting it to be Max. Instead, it's Sam Thompkins. He texted Ava: She's agreed to sign. Meet at 8 A.M. at the property to finalize the paperwork. See you tomorrow.

"Oh my god!" Ava shrieks. Her mood has shifted significantly with just this one text.

"What is it?" Lucy asks. She can't keep up with Ava's range of emotions.

"She's agreed to sign. The squatter."

Lucy looks confused.

"Max and I agreed to offer her twenty-five thousand to incentivize her to vacate the property," Ava clarifies. "She's agreed to take the money. Oh, Thank God!"

Lucy tries to hide the pure terror that is pulsating down her body. "Oh! Who knew it would be that easy?"

"Well, I wouldn't say it's been easy, but now it's finally done. Now I can finally go home."

"Yes, you can finally go home," Lucy replies with just a hint of melancholy.

"I just need to meet with the real estate developer before heading home. I wonder if I can have him come to the property tomorrow morning after we sign everything." Ava says, thinking out loud.

"Real estate developer?"

"Yeah, this big-time developer wants to buy the property. He plans on using the seventy some acres to build a waterfront condo community."

"You're selling? Why would you sell?" Lucy asks a bit too aggressively. She tries to hide her anger, but it's quickly bubbling to the surface.

"You didn't think I was going to keep the property, did you?"

"This is your family history. I don't know. I guess I thought you'd want to hang on to it."

Ava shakes her head, "This isn't my history. My history and legacy is in London. This was something I never really knew. A mere memory, that's all. "

Before Lucy can rebuke that statement, Ava opens the car door.

"Thank you so much for the ride and being such a listening ear. I'm so sorry to have unloaded all of that onto you."

Lucy waves her off as if it was no big deal. In reality, this was a huge deal. It was an earth-shattering kind of deal.

Just as Ava is about to close the car door, she adds, "Oh, and if you don't mind, can we keep what I told you today between us? I would greatly appreciate it."

"Of course. What's another secret, right?" Lucy says, smirking.

Ava gives a nervous, soft-closed smile. "Right." She whispers as she shuts the car door.

Lucy backs out of the parking lot and heads South. She's not going into work today. She has something much more important that just came up.

———————

TESSA

Tommy is sitting on my couch, giving me a speech about why I should settle with her. He's coming up with all the reasons why negotiating with Ava would be a bad idea. Tommy is all too quick to be the peacemaker. He's been in the middle of the countless of fights I've had with my parents. I can't count the number of times he's begged me to apologize. I have a fiery streak in me. When it gets ignited, it's tough to put out. Deep down, I know I was a bandaid fix for my adoptive parents. At six years old, their birth daughter, Layla, died of Leukemia. They adopted me just six months after Layla's death. I've always felt my entire childhood was spent living in the shadow of Layla and what could have been.

"I just really think you need to be smart here," Tommy says.

"I am being smart. Don't you know you never take the first deal offered?" Tessa fires back.

"Twenty-five grand is a lot of money, Tessa."

"No shit, Sherlock. I know she's holding out. I know we can get her to come up more."

"Tessa, this is her deceased parents' house. Not only is she the rightful owner, but she's also being kind and giving you a gift. Take the gift."

"What do you even know about this chick? Kind? I've seen anything but kind, thank you very much." Tessa says, holding her ground, "Plus, I have the right to be here too. I looked it up online and I have at least thirty days to produce the paperwork to prove my residency here."

"Why are you fighting this so hard? What is this land to you besides a nice waterfront rental unit?"

Tessa sighs. She owes it to Tommy to finally admit how she acquired the property. After her parents and Tommy kicked her out, Tessa had nowhere to turn. She didn't want to admit to Tommy that she'd been sleeping out of her car during the dead of winter. To admit how a woman in AA started to notice and offered her this piece of land to live on, almost free of charge. A handshake deal. No papers. No expiration date. At first, Tessa thought the woman was playing some sort of sick joke on her. Soon,

she realized this woman was dead serious. To this day,

Tessa has never seen that woman again, not at AA or

anywhere in Chestertown. She still can't figure out why the

woman gave her the land to live on, but she's not in any

place to question the legitimacy of it. An opportunity is an

opportunity. She's no dummy. But now this Ava woman is

threatening to take the property from her. Tessa can't quite

bear the fact that she'll have to start back at square one.

Tessa has carried an immense amount of guilt after

her adopted father passed away from Parkinson's last year.

She blames herself for her father's death. While he was sick

with Parkinson's for over ten years, she knows her accident

with the school bus sent her father over the edge. After that

whole nightmare of a situation, her father's health took a

turn for the worse and he never quite recovered. While

Tommy would never admit it, Tessa knows he harbors

some resentment towards her for her part in it all. That's

why she's spent the last year desperately trying to clean up the mess that she'd made. That's why she agreed to let Tommy accompany her to all her AA meetings. She wants nothing more than to get her relationship with Tommy back on track.

As if reading her mind, Tommy grabs Tessa's hands in his. "Please, Tessa. Just take the money. I can help you rebuild. I will be with you every step of the way."

Tessa wipes the tears from her eyes, which haven't stopped flowing since she told Tommy everything. She's tired. She's tired of running from reality. It's finally caught up with her.

"Ok, Tommy. Ok."

———————

LUCY

Of course I kept tabs on Tessa. I kept tabs on both Tessa and Ava. It was part of the deal. I knew I had to step in when I noticed Tessa sleeping out of her car for weeks on end. Did I want to step in? No, of course not. Ava had been in London for almost a decade. Tessa was in and out of rehab living with her adoptive parents. Everything and everyone were in their rightful places. But I had to step in. I'm not completely heartless, after all. I saw the property on Happy Hollow as a way of remediating the past. Not all of it. No, I could never remediate the entire past. That was clear with each year that passed. Giving Tessa the property was the right thing to do. The only thing to do in my mind. But now it's all gone to shit. This property can't be sold. It would open up pandoras fucking box. So now I must make the call I've dreaded making for twenty-five years. He won't be hard to reach, but he'll be hard to find. As if I don't have enough on my plate already...

AVA

Ava is driving along Happy Hollow Road, sipping a piping hot coffee and grinning from ear to ear. It's been so long since she slept that well. Finally, a peaceful, uninterrupted sleep. She could rest knowing that today is the day she can escort Tessa off the property and fly home to London. All of this mess will be behind her. She couldn't secure a meeting with the developers today, which was a bummer, but she can always do a virtual meeting in a few weeks. This property isn't going anywhere. The last thing Ava wants to do is fly all the way back to this town. She'd be ecstatic if she never had to return to Chestertown again.

Ava is almost at the property's front gates when she notices a familiar car. Lucy's Honda is parked alongside the front gate, blocking the entrance.

Ava parks her rental car off to the side. She's beyond confused.

"Lucy?" Ava says as she climbs down from the SUV, "Wait. What the heck are you doing here?"

Ava remembers telling Lucy about the property and the squatter, but she's positive she never revealed the actual address.

Lucy calmly steps closer to Ava, "Ava...we should talk."

"Talk about what? How did you even find this place?" Ava asks, still utterly confused.

"Ava, how quickly you forget. I'm far more resourceful than you give me credit for."

"Forgive me, but I'm not understanding."

"Didn't I always teach you to trust your instincts?" Lucy sighs, "You've grown soft in London."

Ava's heart drops. She's starting to realize this visit is no coincidence after all. This was planned.

"What is this about? What do you want?"

Lucy crosses her arms across her chest. "What do I want or what do I need?"

"Lucy. Enough of this charade. What do you need?"

"I need you to get back into your car, return to London, and never set foot in this town again."

Ava motions to the front gate where Lucy is standing, "I'm trying to do just that, but someone seems to be blocking the entrance."

"You can't sell this property," Lucy says.

"Oh really?" Ava scoffs, "Pretty sure you have no say in this. I can do whatever I want with this property. It's mine. Remember?"

"You don't want me to do this. Trust me."

"Do what? What are you after? What's your angle here? Do you want money? Was all this chumminess just a ploy because you were using me? How much money do you want?"

"I said I need you to get out of here," Lucy repeats, enunciating each syllable.

Ava digs her feet deeper into the ground. She's not running from this. Not this time. "Let me be very clear here. You are not getting any piece of this property. I will gladly leave here once you let me inside those gates to sign the papers."

Lucy grabs her phone from her back pocket, "You always have to make things so difficult, don't you."

Lucy hands over her phone to Ava.

Ava looks down at the screen and her face goes stark white.

She's looking at a picture of her and Tommy standing out on the back deck of the property. He has his hand on the small of her back. She flips to another picture that shows Tommy helping Ava onto the boat at the marina. She flicks over to the final image. It's of her and Tommy at the oyster farm. The image is blurry, but if you look hard enough, you can see Ava and Tommy standing no more than an inch apart, locked in an embrace.

Ava drops the phone and backs away a few steps.

"What the hell is this?"

Lucy points to the phone on the ground. "This is you being sloppy. Wouldn't you agree, Ava?"

"I opened up to you. I trusted you. But now I see I was just being used as a pawn in some sick little game you're playing."

"Like I said, you left me no choice."

"You need to leave this property immediately."

"Ava. I need you to understand this very clearly." Lucy picks up the phone from the ground and brushes off the dust. "These pictures will be sent to Max Greenfield if you decide to sell this property."

"Why are you doing this?" Ava asks, her voice croaking. She's trying so hard to be strong.

"This is just business. It's nothing personal."

"How much money do you want?"

Lucy laughs, "As if money could make this all go away."

"Please. Just tell me how much you want. What's your number?"

"You're not understanding. There is no number. You need to leave this town and this property as it is. No selling anything. That is what it will take for me not to send those pictures."

There is a moment of silence between the two women as Ava sorts through this in her mind. Ava is furious with herself. She should have known better than to let Lucy Gonzalez, of all people, waltz back into her life. The very woman who once taught her to build a fortress around her heart took one swing and sent the whole wall crumbling down. It was that easy.

Ava walks past Lucy and opens the gate. "You don't scare me. Not anymore. All you are and ever have been is a bully. It's sad, really, when you think about it. Nothing ever came of your life. You're still here in this no-name town rotting away. I actually feel bad for you."

Ava opens the door to the gate so she's fully inside the lines of the property. She slams the gates shut so Lucy is locked out on the other side.

"Go ahead and send those pictures. I dare you." Ava is seething now. "I'm not going to ask you again. Get the hell off my property before I call the police."

Ava turns on her heels and heads towards the house, willing herself not to look back. As soon as she hears Lucy's car start up, she lets out the breath she'd been holding.

AVA

I knew I was taking a huge gamble trying to call Lucy's bluff. I've never been any good at poker. Max is the true card shark. His love for poker has morphed into an obsession that some would very much call a gambling addiction. I try to ignore the fact that our once hefty lump sum of savings seems to be quickly dwindling. It's not my money, after all. I don't have a say in any of it, do I? Max had a cushiony trust fund that liquified when he turned thirty. Over the past five years, Max has been slowly draining the fund. Turns out, his gambling addiction has turned into a very real problem. One I can no longer turn a blind eye to. I confronted Max about it a few months ago. He shut it down real quick. He made it crystal clear that the money was his money to spend how he pleases. So much for marriage being fifty-fifty, huh? While I have a successful career, most of my initial paychecks went to paying off the impressive debt I accrued. I lost count of how many credit cards I'd opened over the years. When I checked our joint bank account last night, it was clear Max has been having quite the spending bender while I've been away. This property is becoming more and more valuable the more nights I spend away from London. This is precisely why I need to sell this land and get out of here as soon as possible. But those pictures. How in the hell did Lucy get those? She must have been following me. How naive of me to think after all these years she'd changed. She's always had a motive, that one. She's right. I have grown soft in London. I still have it in me, though. I'm a fighter. That never leaves you, no matter how hard you try to run from it. I have no time to be paranoid. I need to sign these papers. My flight back to London leaves in five hours. I know Lucy says she doesn't want money, but she's making minimum wage as a maid at the DoubleTree. I will make her an offer she can't refuse. Everyone has a number. It's just about finding out what that number is.

Ava hands the pen to Tessa.

Tessa, Ava, and Tommy are all silently sitting at the kitchen table as Sam hands out the paperwork. Ava was immediately uneasy at the sight of Tommy. She just wants to erase that time on the boat from her memory. She plans to act as if nothing happened yesterday and she sure hopes Tommy does the same.

"I forgot to ask if you wanted a copy," Sam says, filling the silence in the room

"Definitely not," Tessa replies. She pushes the signed papers back across the table to Sam.

Tommy places his hand on Tessa's shoulder, "She would like a copy."

Tessa shoots Tommy a look but relaxes. She knows he's only looking out for her best interest.

"Fine. Yes, please send over a copy."

Tommy and Ava are staring at one another as if they're trying to break the record for the world's longest staring contest.

Finally, Sam Thompkins interrupts the awkwardness. "Well, that should be all for today, folks." He lets out a pitiful laugh. No one else makes a peep. "I'll have our office send over the copies this afternoon. Thank you for coming today, and please don't hesitate to reach out if you have any other questions. I'm always here."

Ava chimes in, "Yes, thank you for coming today. I wish you all the best."

She sticks out her hand, but Tessa declines to shake it.

"Do you really mean that?" Tessa asks.

Ava pauses. Does she really mean that? While Tessa has made what was supposed to be a short trip extremely difficult, she truly wishes Tessa well. She hopes she can clean up her act and get better. What's the saying, never kick a dog when it's down?

"I do mean that," Ava answers honestly. She nods a farewell and turns for the door. She's almost at the gates when she hears her name.

"Ava!" Tommy is running to catch up with her.

Ava has no other option but to stop and turn around to face him.

"Please, Ava, just hear me out for a second,"

Tommy says.

"Tommy, I'm sorry. I have to get to the airport. I'm going to miss my flight."

"Are you really just going to forget about this?"

"Forget about what? Nothing happened, Tommy. It was a fleeting moment. That's it. Please don't make this into something more than it is. Please." Ava begs.

Tommy looks back at Ava like he's just been crushed into a thousand pieces. Maybe what happened between the two of them would have been something in another lifetime, but not in this lifetime. Ava needs to focus on getting back to London and getting home.

Ava turns back around and crosses the threshold of the iron gates, praying this is the last time she will have to walk through these busted gates. She starts the car, leaving

Tommy and Happy Hollow in her rearview. A piece of her

heart breaks for reasons she can't quite put into words.

———————

LUCY

Lucy's car is parked at the end of Happy Hollow

Road, right behind a big tree. It's parked so that no one can

see her, but she has a clear view of the front entrance.

Once she sees Ava's car turn right onto the main

highway, she dials a number that she seems to have

memorized.

The call almost goes to voicemail, but someone

picks up on the last ring.

"It's me," Lucy says to the person on the other end

of the line. "We've got a problem."

———————

AVA

Ava hands the car keys over to the man at the rental car kiosk.

She looks down at her phone. She has exactly one hour until her flight boards. That should be enough time to get through security and grab a quick bite.

She notices a little bell notification on her phone that she didn't see this morning. It's a voicemail. She prays it's not Sam Thompkins or, even worse, Tessa or Tommy. She's initially relieved when she hears Max's voice. However, relief quickly turns to panic in the short span of twenty seconds.

Max's voice is stern. She remains motionless at the front door of the rental car company as she listens to each word carefully. Max is telling Ava not to come home. Max is describing the pictures he received from an unsolicited source. He's not asking Ava if it's actually her in the pictures because he knows the truth. Ava saw the pictures herself. There's no way she can deny it even if she tried.

It's her. It's as clear as day. He's explaining how he needs time to process this all. He needs time to decide what he's going to do.

And just like that, one of the hinges on the door to her past breaks wide open.

———————

TESSA

Tessa is tapping her foot incessantly as she sits in the waiting room. Tommy reaches over and places his large hand on Tessa's knee to steady her.

The waiting room at BrightSide rehab facility is all too familiar. Tessa has been through this song and dance before. She undoubtedly knows the questions awaiting her on the other side of this room. She also knows the slew of rules that will be slung at her in an attempt to scare her shitless.

"It's gonna be ok, Tess, I promise," Tommy says as he squeezes her knee.

Tessa nods.

She's agreed to a two-week stay this time. The goal is to move in with Tommy afterward and help him run the oyster farm. It's not the most enticing opportunity, but Tessa knows she's in no position to negotiate. Tommy has even generously fronted this entire production. He wants Tessa to save the twenty-five thousand. He wants to ensure she has the savings to fall back on once she's out.

Tessa places her hand over the top of her brother's hand, "I'm gonna be okay, Tommy. I'm going to try this time. Really try."

Unlike all the other times she's said this, she actually believes it this time. She will try. She will try not only for herself but also for Tommy. She can't let him down. He's given everything to help Tessa make something of her life and she's realizing she just may want to start making something of her life, too. Maybe she'll be a chef

or run a bakery shop like she's always dreamt of doing.

Whatever it is, it won't have the word addict attached to it.

Not this time.

AVA

Blood. So much blood. It's dripping like little rain

pellets off of Ava's arms. Her entire white T-shirt is now

soaked in a very dark amber-red. She tries to wipe it away,

but she can't move fast enough. There's too much blood.

Someone is crying, but Ava can't determine if it's her or

someone else. And then there is silence. A silence so still it

rattles your eardrums. And then everything goes black.

Ava jumps up from her seat. She looks around.

She's still at the airport, sitting in baggage claim.

After she received the voicemail from Max, she sat

in the baggage claim area for hours, weighing her options.

She could fly home to London and sort this all out with Max in person. She would make him see that this was all just some sort of misunderstanding. He would forgive her. He'd have to forgive her, right? But no, his message was resoundingly clear. He needs time to process it all. So, she's left with the only other option. The most terrible option of them all. She turns the key over and over in her hands. Her gel nail polish is starting to chip off on her middle finger. The irony is not lost on her. It's like the universe is giving her one giant middle finger. Finally, she collects her suitcase and purse. She heads back outside the baggage claim doors, towards the very last place on earth she wants to be. But first, she has to make a quick pit stop.

Ava is sitting across from the manager at the DoubleTree hotel as she irately explains to him how one of his employees has stolen her thirty-thousand-dollar Rolex watch from her room. A watch that Ava strategically placed in her bra just before entering the doors of the DoubleTree.

To be honest, Ava finds the watch quite obnoxious, but Max notices when she 'forgets' to wear it. Ava thinks the idea of spending thirty thousand dollars on any piece of jewelry is utterly absurd. She has to remember that thirty thousand dollars to Max is just a drop in the ocean. An ocean that seems to be slowly drying up with each night Max fancies himself 'just one hand' at the casino. Ava continues to give a very detailed description of the maid who has been tending to her room. It's a description that leaves no room for interpretation. The manager seems surprised, telling Ava that Lucy Gonzalez is his most trusted and loyal employee. It takes only the mere mention of a lawsuit for the manager to assure Ava that the appropriate actions will be taken. Two can play this game, Ava thinks. Bring it on Lucy Gonzalez. Bring. It. On.

———————

LUCY

He was not happy about the newest developments. It's been so long since he's heard from me. We both thought this was all sealed in the past, where it belongs. He's upped the ante on everything. He wants me to finish this. I was trying to let Ava off easy. I really was. I didn't want to ruin yet another life. But after that stint she pulled at my place of work, she deserves everything she's about to have coming to her. The gloves are off.

Lucy dials a number on her phone. When no one picks up she leaves a voicemail. "Baby, it's me. Call me when you can. I'm heading to Carpaccio's for dinner. Let me know if you want me to pick up your favorite. I can also get Elisa that tiramisu she loves so much. Call me back when you can. Love you."

Lucy ends the call. She scrolls through her call log. There are at least twenty outgoing calls to the same number that have never been returned.

Lucy's daughter, Patty, stopped talking to her about two years ago. The restraining order has yet to be lifted. The order was put in place after Lucy was caught stealing money from Patty. Patty confronted Lucy about it and things got physical. Lucy didn't mean for things to get physical, but she was backed into a corner. She did what she always does when she's backed into a corner: she fought back.

AVA

Ava looks down at the empty bottle of wine sitting on her lap. Maybe she and Tessa aren't so different after all, she thinks. She's sitting out back on the deck of the Happy Hollow property. It's a chilly fall evening and she has a thin blanket draped over her thighs.

She grabs her head. It's already throbbing from all the wine. She's been steadily refilling her glass ever since she arrived back on the property this afternoon. She's confident the only way she'll get an ounce of sleep tonight is if she's mind-numbingly wasted.

Ava stands up in search of the second bottle of wine she purchased from the local gas station. The most expensive bottle in the store was twenty bucks. No wonder her head is already throbbing, she thinks. Ava's foot lands in the hole of one of the broken floorboards. She goes flying face-first into the deck. She has just enough time to stick her hands out to brace her fall.

"FUCK!" Ava screams. She tries to pull her leg free from the floorboard with no luck. "AHHHHHHHHH."

She screams and screams until her leg finally gets loose.

Ava's all rage and fury now. She picks up the shovel propped against the deck and starts swinging. She's a tornado on a destructive path. Down goes part of the weathered railing. She swings at the empty bird feeder hanging by the window that overlooks the deck. It goes flying toward the water.

"Fuck you! Fuck all of you! FUCKKKKKKK YOUUUU!!!!!!" Ava winds up and slams the shovel into the deck, knocking out four floorboards.

She throws the shovel aside and grabs her hands. That last swing caused a wave of pain to pulsate through her hands. She's bent over now, completely out of breath.

"I'd hate to see the other guy."

Ava whips around to see Tommy standing on the steps.

"For what it's worth, you've got a pretty stellar swing." Tommy continues.

"How long have you been here?" Ava asks, mortified.

"Long enough to know not to ever fuck with you."

Ava laughs. She can't help but laugh. At him. At her. At the sheer absurdity of all of this.

"I probably look like I've lost my marbles."

"It looked quite cathartic if I'm being honest. Maybe I should give it a try."

"Something going on in your world where you would need to demolish an entire deck?"

"What's not going on is the better question," Tommy replies with an intriguing vagueness. "I didn't expect to see you here."

"I could say the same thing to you."

"Tessa wanted me to grab a couple of items that she left behind in the move."

"She could have come here to get them. I know she thinks I'm a monster, but I would have let her grab them."

"She's in rehab," Tommy spits out.

"Oh, I see."

Tommy takes a seat without asking. Ava is surprisingly relieved that he wants to linger a bit longer to chat. Being alone on this property, especially as it starts to get dark, is unnerving.

"Yeah. I don't know why, but her attempt to get clean feels different this time."

Ava pauses. She knows she probably shouldn't open this door with Tommy, but she has no reason not to. At this point, everything has gone to shit. What's one more thing? He wants to talk to someone, and she always has been a great listener.

"Different, how?" Ava asks.

"It's hard to explain it, but something about the look in her eyes – I saw a light in those eyes. A light that I thought had been distinguished long, long ago. It gave me hope."

Hearing Tommy be so vulnerable about his adopted sister is stirring something up within the deep crevices of Ava's heart. She often wished for another sibling and resented her parents for being an only child. After the accident, she prayed and prayed that one of her blood relatives would come forward to save her. She knew her grandparents on her dad's side had been dead for years. She didn't know much about her mother's parents or really anything about her mother's family, for that matter. From what Ava could gather, her mother's family didn't approve of her marriage to her father. They didn't even attend the wedding. All forms of communication had been cut off well before Ava came into the picture.

"I thought you'd be thirty thousand feet in the air somewhere over the Atlantic by now," Tommy comments, changing the subject.

"You and me both," Ava replies. How does she even begin to explain this cluster fuck to Tommy? "There's some issues back home. It was best for me to stay here a few extra days to let the dust settle."

Ava leaves it at that. She prays Tommy doesn't pry any further. The last thing she needs right now is to talk about the elephant in the room.

Tommy nods, picking up on her curtness.

"Do you want some meatloaf?" Ava asks before he has a chance to head inside to fetch Tessa's things.

"Do I want some meatloaf?" Tommy echoes. He has a slightly upturned smirk on his face.

"I got an absurd amount of meatloaf at the grocery store today. Like an embarrassingly absurd amount of meatloaf."

Tommy is now smiling with all his teeth. His left dimple has emerged from its hiding spot. "Well, sign me up for an absurd amount of meatloaf. An embarrassingly absurd amount of meatloaf is what we shall have."

Ava laughs from deep within her belly. It feels good to laugh after the last twelve hours she's had.

Tommy follows her inside, and for once, Ava does not dread being inside the four walls of this house.

———————

LUCY

Lucy is parked alongside a narrow street lined with modest middle-class houses. She is staring across the street at a blue-shuttered house with a beautiful blue-striped awning shading a deep porch.

Lucy knows she shouldn't be here, but she doesn't know where else to turn. Everything is a mess. She's tried to keep the order for so long, but the cracks have split wide open. The first crack formed that awful night when Lucy was babysitting Patty's daughter, Elisa. Patty wasn't supposed to be home yet. It was just a few hundred bucks. Patty and her high brow financier husband, Eric, had more than enough money to pass around. So what if Lucy had been taking some money here and there? In Patty's world, this was merely chump change. What was the big deal?

Lucy didn't mean to push Patty, but she didn't know what else to do. Patty came charging at her like a bull. Her daughter is a towering figure. It was frightening. If only she knew then that one push would lead to two years of hell. Two years of being shunned by her own family. Two years of repentance. Two years of not being able to see her granddaughter. Two years of the law telling her she must always stay at least one hundred yards away from Patty and her family at all times.

There's a knock on Lucy's car door.

Shit, Lucy thinks. It's Patty's husband, Eric. Lucy knows Eric is behind all of this. He must be. Patty would never take it to this extreme measure. She would never let two years go by without speaking to her own mother. This must be all Eric's doing.

Lucy rolls down the window.

"What are you doing here?" Eric asks. He's a tiny specimen of a human. He can't be one centimeter over 5'4". Lucy is convinced he has Napoleon syndrome.

"I just want to see Patty," Lucy replies meekly.

Eric sighs, "You shouldn't be here. You know you shouldn't be here."

"Please, Eric. It's been two years. I just want five minutes with her. That's it." Lucy knows the response that is sure to come next. It's the same one they always give her. Usually, Eric politely tells Lucy that Patty doesn't want to see her. He then, not so politely, asks her to leave.

Instead, Eric says something that shocks Lucy to her core. "Come back tomorrow at five."

Lucy almost lets out a wail, "Thank you!"

Eric raises his hands. "I'm not promising anything. I'll see what I can do, but I'm not promising anything."

Lucy nods. She stopped listening to Eric. All she can think about now is finally being able to see Patty and Elisa. Finally.

Lucy puts the car in drive and allows a smile to slowly creep in. It's the first time she has smiled, really smiled, in over two years.

———————

TESSA

The first-timers are so easy to spot. They come into places like this all bright-eyed and bushy-tailed. They are all too full of hope and buy so easily into the jargon and facade. They think they've hit rock bottom and are genuinely grateful to begin climbing out. Little do they know, rock bottom is a bottomless pit not even the best mountaineer can climb out of.

"Tessa?" A man with deep olive skin and dark brown eyes intently stares at her. It's making her uncomfortable.

"I'm sorry?" Tessa asks. She was not listening. She was tuning him out like she does with all the other countless workers at this place. Their cheeriness is nauseating.

"When was the day of your last menstrual cycle?" The Greek goddess of a specimen repeats.

She should be embarrassed, but she's learned to swallow her pride in a place like this. They've seen it all. Nothing phases anyone in this place. "Ummmm. I think it's been at least eighteen months."

The man puts down his pen and paper. "Tessa, can I be frank with you?"

"I don't know, can you?" Tessa loves nothing more than to answer their questions with another question. It drives them crazy.

"Look, I can give you some bullshit copasetic answer right now to make you feel like you'll be okay, but that's not who I am." The psychologist removes his glasses and shifts his position on his chair, "I'm going to give you the facts. Take with them what you will, but I will not lie to you."

Tessa swallows hard. She's caught off guard by this man. She's used to the fluffy intake doctors who assure her that she will be at the pinnacle of health by the time she leaves this place. If she ever leaves this place, she thinks.

"If you don't start gaining weight, you will die," he continues without adding an ounce of fluff.

Tessa is too stunned to speak. She knows she's lost some weight. She sees the way people try to look away when she's out walking in public. She knows her clothes hang off of her body, but she didn't really think it had gotten that bad.

The Greek goddess continues, "Your organs will shut down with malnutrition. That or cirrhosis of the liver will take you out. It's as simple as that."

Tessa's gut reaction is to tell this beautiful man with a clipboard to fuck right off. Who is he to comment on her body? But she stops herself. In the weirdest of ways, she finds his unfiltered words refreshing. This is the first time someone has spoken to her without kid gloves on. Her entire life, she's been handed around like fine china and talked about in hushed tones. People take one look at her and assume she can't handle the hard conversations. But here she is now with this devilishly handsome man who is telling her the worst of the worst. And she's still standing. This man sees her. Finally, she thinks.

"Thank you," Tessa replies. She gets up from the sterile metal chair. "Your honesty is beyond appreciated."

Ava exits the doctor's room feeling more invigorated and alive than she's felt in all her twenty-some years. She can handle this. All of this. She's so much stronger than even she gives herself credit for. If that's not something to feel alive about, she doesn't know what is. She's flirting with death and has never felt more alive. What a beautiful juxtaposition.

LUCY

Lucy uses the big brass knocker on Patty's door to alert the forces of her presence. She's praying this isn't some big practical joke. She half expects Eric to open the door and scream GOTCHA! before slamming the door in her face. But Patty opens the door and steps aside to let her mother inside. This is the first time Lucy's been inside the house since that fateful night. Lucy takes in the cosmetic changes they've made to the entryway. It's a different shade of periwinkle, she thinks.

Lucy refrains herself from enveloping her daughter in the biggest bear hug. She knows she's not ready for that. Baby steps. Lucy has to crawl before she can walk again.

Patty guides her mom to the bright sunroom at the back of the house. Their expansive and perfectly manicured lawn glistens in the waning sun.

They both sit on the chunky Restoration Hardware chairs that face the backyard. Lucy still can't believe how much money they spent furnishing this place with high-end designer brands. It's a lifestyle so far removed from the thrift store bargain basement that Patty was raised in.

"I would offer you something to drink, but I'm confident this won't take long."

Lucy did not expect this, especially so soon after entering the house. Patty's body language is scaring her.

"Patty…"

Patty doesn't let her finish. "Do you actually know how much you stole from us, Mom?"

"Patty, please don't speak to me like that," Lucy replies. She can't believe her daughter is still this up in arms about a few hundred dollars. "Haven't you punished me enough?"

"Thirty thousand dollars."

"What!?"

"Do you need me to say it again?"

Thirty thousand dollars? Surely it can't be that much, Lucy thinks. The safe that Patty gave her the code for was for emergency use only. It had almost two hundred thousand dollars in there. Lucy was careful not to take too much, wasn't she? She took only what she needed and never more. She knew her daughter would understand. Yet, here her daughter is, not being so understanding after all.

"Thirty thousand dollars. We could have used that thirty thousand dollars for Elisa's education – for my continuing education – for a new furnace system. For anything we wanted, really, because it was our money. But now it's gone."

Lucy can't believe this is happening. She refuses to believe this to be the truth.

"Instead, you chose to spend this money on yet another one of your floozy junkie boyfriends or on God knows what else." Patty continues.

It's true. Rodrigo was quite convincing with his business proposition this time. Lucy believed she could return the money (with interest!) back to the safe without anyone noticing. How the hell did they even know the money was missing? Lucy convinced herself that Rodrigo would finally be the one who would stay. He said all the right things. He made their future together seem so bright and real. He didn't even ask for the money upfront like all the others. He played the long game. It wasn't until about seven months into dating that he started planting the seed. He was good. Ultimately, he made it seem like it was

Lucy's idea and not his. But he left, just like all the others. They always leave.

"I will pay it back to you." Lucy is almost whispering. She's terrified to say the wrong thing that will send this terrible conversation over the edge to the point of no return.

"At this point, it's not even about the money! Christ!" Patty stands up from her seat. She's visibly had it. "You pushed me! You physically assaulted me!"

Lucy stands up now too, mirroring her daughters body language, "That is quite dramatic, don't you think? You charged me! I was scared!" Lucy quickly sits back down. The last thing she wants is for this to escalate like it did that night.

"I'm your daughter. Your daughter!" Patty says through her tears, "I just want to shake you! You've always been money-hungry, but these past few years, it's just become like a disease inside you. This rotting evil."

Lucy knows her daughter knows nothing about evil. She hasn't come face to face with evil. Lucy has. She's protected her daughter from evil. She's sheltered her from evil. How dare she come at her like this after all she's done for her?

"I've fought so damn hard for you to have a good life," Lucy retorts back.

"Ha! Good life!?" Patty scoffs. "You mean one where we sleep out of tents or crash on your latest boyfriends couch for months on end. Only to get evicted in the middle of the night? Yeah, some wonderful life, Mom."

"Don't you dare!" Lucy can't believe this is happening. Why is her daughter doing this to her?

"The cycle ends now, Mom. You need to leave."

Lucy stands back up and opens up her arms. She's desperate. She tries to find the words that are choking in her throat.

"Please, don't do this, baby."

Patty shows her to the door. "Please go. Now."
Patty's words are firm and final. It's clear she's not
budging.

Lucy sighs. She's paddling without an oar upstream.
She knows when her daughter has made up her mind. It's
done.

"I will pay you back," Lucy whispers again one
final time before the front door is curtly closed in her face.

Lucy stands there for a minute and lets it all soak in.
She will make this right. She will make it right if it's the
last thing she does. Otherwise, what is the point of living?
Patty and Elisa are all she has. She knows Patty said it's not
about the money, but everyone has a number. Even Patty.
And even Lucy. Which is precisely what she will tell him
tomorrow morning. Her number. The number to make this
all right with Patty. And then some.

———————

AVA

Ava's eyes flutter open. She peeks out of her right eye, relieved she's in her bedroom. Technically, she's in what used to be her parent's bedroom. She's hit with the reality that she's all too quick to try and forget. This is all hers now. This land, this house, and even this bed. Speaking of, she needs to change these sheets. Lord knows who has been sleeping on these sheets and in what condition. Gross. She recoils from the bed just thinking about it.

She steadies herself and looks into the oval mirror that has sand dollars glued onto all four corners. It's the kind of cheeky decor you would see in a beach house. Anywhere else it would come off as tacky but here, in this house, it feels almost nostalgic.

Ava squints her eyes, focusing on the bottom left corner of the mirror. There's a chip on one of the sand dollars. Maybe it fell and caused one of the sand dollars to break in two, she thinks.

Before Ava can think of a more rational explanation, it all comes rushing in. Just how it always does when the memories of her past resurface from a faraway land.

Little Ava is looking into the sand dollar mirror. She has bright cherry red lipstick on. She's smacking her lips, sloppily spreading the lipstick all around. A beautiful woman with golden blonde hair and bronzed skin looks back at Ava in the mirror. This woman seems so familiar. It's not her mother, but she can't quite place this woman. She's too far out of reach for Ava to grasp from her memory bank. She looks very young, as if she could be Ava's babysitter. But no, that doesn't feel right either. This woman isn't a stranger, though. Ava knows that much.

"You look like Marilyn Monroe! All the boys won't be able to resist you!" The cheery blonde says to Ava.

Ava smiles. Some of the lipstick is stuck on her teeth. It's so absurdly ridiculous. Both Ava and the blonde erupt into a fit of laughter. A laughter that is cut short by the presence of her dad hovering over the doorway.

"What are you doing?" Ava's dad asks. It's a question mostly directed toward the blonde.

The blonde gawks, "It's just a bit of makeup, Jeff. Don't make a big deal of this."

Ava's dad turns to her with blackened eyes. His eyes are scaring Ava. She's never seen those eyes before. "Go get that crap off your face."

"But Dad! Please!" Ava replies.

Before Ava can understand what's happening, her dad grabs a candle holder sitting on the dresser and chucks it toward the blonde. She ducks, and the candle holder crashes into the bottom right corner of the sand dollar mirror. A massive chunk of the sand dollar goes flying onto the ground.

Ava's crying and not just because of her dad's reaction. She liked that mirror. Her mom spent hours gluing all those sand dollars to the mirror. Where is her mom? Surely she would have heard the loud crash that just ensued, Ava thinks. Her mom will fix this. She needs to find her mom.

"You ready?"

Ava is once again jolted back to reality. Tommy is standing at the entrance of her bedroom. He's cleaned up quite nicely. He's sporting a pair of linen slacks and a Tommy Bahama short-sleeved button-down shirt.

"Are we late?" Ava asks.

"Not if you hurry."

Last night, over a shit load of meatloaf and cheap wine, Tommy asked Ava if she wanted to go to the annual Chestertown fish fry festival. It's an event held at a local farm that you can only get to by boat. Ava agreed. How could she not agree after the intimate conversation she had last night with Tommy? She was a blubbering mess as she told him her story. She wasn't even sure she even had an actual story to tell. It was more like a hurricane of starts and stops that somehow led her to this moment. She divulged every detail. She told Tommy about her parent's accident, the Catholic orphanage, the handful of foster families that came and went, and, of course, her marriage to Max. She even told Tommy about the voicemail she received from Max right before she was about to board her flight back to London. She strategically left out why Max needed some time apart. Ava didn't want to involve anyone else in Lucy's threats. Besides, she was confident she could handle Lucy Gonzalez herself. A tiger doesn't change its stripes, although it may add a few extra stripes as the years drag on. Ava is prepared now. Because what tigers seem to be most afraid of is their own shadow.

A flush of embarrassment courses through Ava's body. Had she asked Tommy anything about himself? Or had she simply just ransacked the entire conversation,

droning on and on about her poor little rich girl life?

Tommy had been such a good listener.

Ava glances over at Tommy. He's starting up the

boat and lugging a large cooler into the Whaler. She

blushes. Those damn back muscles of his really do

something to her. Logically, Ava knows she probably

shouldn't be getting back into the Whaler with Tommy.

Logically, she knows she probably should be taking time

alone to sort this all out in her mind. Logically, she knows

she's thinking quite illogically. She's rolling the dice on her

perfectly curated life. But right now, she's tired of playing

it safe. She's tired of thinking through every possible

scenario as if her life is one big solvable mathematical

equation. At this moment, she just wants to be. She wants

to do what feels right. Tonight, that just so happens to mean

being open to what this shore town has to offer. She's spent

so many years trying to wash off the memories of this

place. Had she ever given Chestertown a chance? This place, for better or worse, is a part of her. Maybe it's time to finally meet this part of her that has been living dormant inside of her all along.

Tommy and Ava are sitting around a huge fire pit in the middle of an open field. There's a man with a large wooden stick who is strategically poking at the fire. He stabs a fish that's being cooked in the middle rack of the pit.

"I guess they really don't call it fish fry for nothing," Ava remarks, watching the man poke at more fish in the middle of the fire pit.

"Poor little fishy," Tommy comments. "Although that fish was pretty amazing."

Ava grabs her stomach in agreement, "Best farm-to-table I've ever had."

"I don't know about the table, but we definitely checked off the farm part," Tommy comments as one of the partygoers walks by with a fish on a stick.

It's certainly not an elegant setting by any means but it has a certain charm to it that Ava finds heartwarming. If this were a party back in London, she would have had to be dressed to the nines and be on her best behavior. Here, she can quite literally kick off her shoes and wear her denim cut-off jean shorts. Max would have been appalled at her outfit choice tonight. The first thing Tommy said to Ava when he saw her was just how much he loved her shorts. He told her she'd picked the perfect outfit for the occasion. Looking around the field, he was right. Effortlessly casual is the best way to describe the patrons who showed up by the masses tonight. There had to be close to two hundred people here and more than fifty boats all anchored in the bay just past the fire pits.

"Thank you for inviting me. This is fun."

Before Tommy has time to reply, his name is being yelled from behind them. Ava turns around just as Tommy is being hoisted in the air by a bowling ball-like man.

"You mother fucker! Not only did you forget to mention you were coming to this thing –" the bowling ball-like man says through a croaky voice, "but you forgot to mention that you were bringing a lady!"

"Must you always manhandle me in public, Tucker? It's embarrassing." Tommy says.

Tucker, the bowling-ball-like figure, laughs and slaps Tommy on his back, "You mean all of the two times a year I see you in public? Where the hell have you been, man?"

Tucker turns to Ava before Tommy has time to reply. He sticks out his hand, "Tucker Montley, nice to meet you."

"Ava Greenfield. Nice to meet you," Ava replies, taking his sweaty, oversized hand in hers.

"How do you know our boy Tommy, Ava?" Tucker asks, getting right to it.

"Oh my God, Tuck. Can you not? We haven't even gotten a beer yet."

"Relax, Tommy! She doesn't have to answer if she doesn't want to!"

"Tommy and I have a mutual acquaintance who introduced us." Ava answers. It's not a total lie. Tessa is their mutual acquaintance and, because of her, they did get introduced. It's not the kind of formal introduction you would expect, but she spares Tucker those details.

"Very nice. You must be special to get him to come to this thing."

Tommy places his hand on Ava's lower back, "Ignore him. I'm gonna go get us some beers. I'll be right back."

"I'll take a Budweiser while you're at it. Thanks, buddy!" Tucker yells at Tommy as he's walking away.

Tommy holds up his middle finger but keeps walking.

Ava smiles politely at Tucker, unsure what to say next.

"Seriously, how'd you get him to come to this thing?" Tucker asks, continuing his interrogation.

"Isn't this a yearly event?"

"It is. But Tommy hasn't been here in over seven years." Tucker says. "He generally avoids any kind of events where he would run into her."

"Her?" Ava asks, her eyebrows raising just a bit. She's definitely intrigued now.

"Oh shit. Probably shouldn't be spilling the beans, but I've also had about eight bud heavy's, so what the hell?" Tucker points to a pregnant woman on the other side of the field. She has long brown hair and is wearing a loose sundress. "It's been so long since Claire broke off the engagement. You think he'd be over it by now, after all this time."

"Engagement?" Ava replies, trying to hide the shock in her eyes, "I didn't realize Tommy had been engaged."

"Oh yeah. Claire broke his damn heart. She broke it off a few months after his dad passed from Parkinson's. Talk about a shitty move. It was a real classless act. I kind of just expected that he would move towns and we'd never see him again, but I also knew he wanted to honor his dad. I knew in his heart of hearts he couldn't sell the oyster farm. I've always felt he's just been stuck here. Like this town has been some sort of prison he can't seem to escape from."

"Wow," Ava says. Ava is realizing there is still so much she doesn't know about Tommy.

"But now he's here, with you, looking – happy," Tucker says, interrupting her thoughts.

They both turn to look at Tommy. He's standing in line for the beers looking carefree as he talks to someone behind him in line.

"I don't know who you are, Ava Greenfield," Tucker continues, "but you must be important to him. Don't take that lightly, darling."

Tucker pats Ava on the shoulder and gives her a parting smile as he runs to catch up with a group heading back toward their anchored boats.

Ava smiles to herself. Happy. Those five little letters make her happier than she's been in quite some time. She does not take that lightly. Not at all.

It's a few hours and a few beers later, and the party is slowly dying off. Throughout the night, Ava learned a lot of new facts about Tommy, including that he was an All-American lacrosse player at Washington College and that he holds the record for the most oysters shucked in under a minute.

Tommy motions toward his boat, "Ready to go?"

"I think all the fish have been fried. I'm tapping out," Ava replies, holding up her hands in defeat.

Tommy smiles as they both wade into the shin-deep water toward Tommy's anchored Whaler. It's one of the last boats anchored in the water. Ava was surprised when Tommy suggested they stay until they were one of the last few stragglers of the night. It had to be close to midnight now.

Tommy helps Ava onto the boat. Just as Ava is about to take her seat, she runs straight into a fishing rod holder that is poking out ever so slightly. Ava grabs her cheek and winces in pain.

"Ah!" Ava cries out.

"Shit!" Tommy says. He hops onto the boat and is at Ava's side within seconds. "Don't move. Let me see it."

Tommy cradles Ava's head in his gruff hands as he examines her cheek and the rest of her face.

"Well, there's no blood, but that cheek is going to be bruised for sure."

Ava remains motionless. She's silently begging Tommy to keep his hands exactly where they are.

"Are you ok?"

Ava barely lets out an audible yes. She's more than okay. She feels the most okay than she's been in a very long time. Tommy goes to pull away, and, as if on instinct, she grabs his hands and holds them still. Right now, in this moment, thoughts of Max are about as far away from Ava's mind as outer space. She's letting herself lean into it. Lean into this moment that just feels right.

Tommy starts caressing her cheek with his thumb. It's such a small but powerful gesture. It's almost as if this tiny gesture is his way of asking permission to keep going. Ava nods her head. Yes, she wants this just as much as he does. Maybe even more than he does.

Tommy leans in painstakingly slow. He's taking his time, memorizing every freckle that traces Ava's oval face. Ava's brain is mush. Nothing is firing upstairs. All she wants is Tommy's lips on hers, but he seems to be playing the long game.

Tommy inches his lips a bit closer so that they are hovering just over Ava's lips. "God, you're so beautiful," Tommy says as he touches Ava's plump lower lip.

There's nothing left for Ava to do besides open her mouth wider to let Tommy fully in. All of him. It's a slow, sensual kiss. It's so very different from their first kiss. Their first kiss was pure madness mixed with lust. This kiss is much softer and somehow much more meaningful. This kiss communicates a desire that has been steadily brewing inside of both of them.

Ava flips Tommy over onto his back. It's a power move. She slips off the straps of her dress and holds her hands up. Tommy happily obliges. He helps lift her dress completely over her head. He tosses it aside in the boat. Her tan bra is just a bit too tight, accentuating her breasts that much more. Tommy hasn't taken his eyes off of them. Ava maneuvers her hands down towards the button of Tommy's shorts. Tommy grabs her hand to stop her.

"Are you sure?" Tommy asks.

"I've been sure since I first kissed you," Ava replies. In reality, Ava's been sure since she first laid eyes on Tommy. The moment he stepped out of his car on Happy Hollow Road, Ava knew she was in trouble. She somehow intuitively knew that Tommy was going to be a part of her life in one way or another. She'd been trying to push him away because she knew he was going to be the thing that would send her perfectly curated life crumbling down. But in this moment, she does not care. Let her life come tumbling down. It's been so tiring trying to hold up the walls for so long.

Ava continues to unbutton Tommy's shorts as he wiggles himself free. She can feel his girth beneath his boxers, primed and ready for Ava's delicate yet determined fingers. Tommy kisses Ava with all his might. As he does so, he unhooks her bra and lets it fall down her trimmed shoulders. He cups Ava's two perfectly shaped breasts in his hands and lets out a soft moan. Ava's breath is quickening. All she is thinking right now is how quickly she can get Tommy inside of her. As if reading her mind, Tommy flips Ava over on her back. He's the one in charge now. It's an experts move that suggests this isn't his first rodeo. Tommy rips off his boxers, and with one swift movement, he thrusts himself inside of her. Ava's world stops. Her orbit is no longer spinning. It's firmly planted in the here and now. They push and pull, almost in rhythm with the tide. The boat rocking back and forth adds a nice sensual touch that they both lose themselves in. It's as if they're not on the boat but rather intertwined underwater like the sea moss that always used to get stuck in Ava's

hair. When they finally come back up for air, all Ava can

see is the bright stars that cover the night sky like a blanket.

It's the most beautiful and transfixing thing she's ever

experienced. If only they could lay here all night and do

this over and over again. If only...

"I think I want you to take me to a fish fry every

day," Ava says, interrupting the silence.

They both laugh. Just off in the distance, one of the

last stragglers starts up their boat.

Ava freezes and looks at Tommy with pure terror.

Tommy jumps up and grabs Ava's bra and t-shirt.

He quickly hands them to her.

"You don't think they saw anything, did you?" Ava

asks. She was clearly in a trance if she didn't even notice or

check to see if they were completely alone.

"No way. And if they did, they had a great show."

Tommy jokes as he wiggles back into his boxers and shorts.

He leaves his T-shirt off as he starts up the Whaler. Watching Tommy maneuver the boat shirtless makes Ava's insides turn to putty.

"That would definitely be a first for me. Dinner and a show." Ava jokes.

"I'm sorry if I took it too far," Tommy meekly replies.

"You didn't take it too far. I wanted this, too. You don't need to apologize for anything."

"Ok," Tommy replies. His demeanor has shifted. "Guess we better head on back. It's getting late."

This statement deflates all the air in Ava's lungs. What just happened between them was pure magic. Did he not feel that too? Did she get caught up in the moment? Was she simply just another feather on his cap? Ava must have misjudged this entire thing. How could she have been so stupid, Ava thinks to herself. This was nothing more

than a good lay. She let her emotions get the best of her,
like always.

Ava takes a seat toward the front of the boat. Her
back is facing Tommy as she stares out into the black
abyss. She's so mortified. She wishes the night sky would
just swallow her up and take her out of her misery.

"Ready?" Tommy asks.

Ava gives him a thumbs-up but says nothing.

Tommy revs up the engine and steers the boat out of
the channel. A few tears fall down Ava's cheeks. The wind
coming off the boat wipes her tears away before she has
time to wipe them away herself.

———————

TESSA

*It started as something harmless. Something to do
to pass the time in this depressing place. I would ask to see
the psychologist - Doctor Carmichael. I would make up*

reasons I needed to see him. It's all too easy to bend the truth in a place like this. Simply echoing those two little words: suicidal thoughts, was more than enough for them to fly you on a broomstick over to his office. It didn't work, though. Doctor Carmichael called my bluff almost as soon as I opened my mouth.

"Why are you really here, Tessa?" Dr. Carmichael asks. His olive skin tone and dark eyes could disarm even the strictest nun.

"What do you mean?" Tessa asks. She's tilting her head in a way meant to be girlishly cute but instead just makes her look like a freaky pantomime. "I told you. I'm having intrusive thoughts."

"You're not having intrusive thoughts."

"Excuse me? How do you know what goes on inside my head?" It would be so easy for Tessa to go off on him. Just as she has done to all the other doctors and psychiatrists she's seen since being in and out of rehab. But for some reason, she just can't do that to this beautiful specimen of a human that sits before her.

"Because I know you. You've gotten away with a lot. No one has ever really put you in your place. Not like you've needed to be. They've let you off the hook because they're afraid one wrong word will send you flying off the handle. But you and I both know this is all just a cry for attention. You want someone, anyone, to finally see you. Truly see you. And I know I'm hitting the mark just by the look in your eyes. Your pupils have grown two sizes since I started talking, which means you're either shocked by my accuracy or turned on by it. Or maybe both. I'm okay with that—especially the latter. I'm not some sick masochistic who gets off on hitting on his patients. I want to be very clear about that. There's just something about you. The people in this place – most of them are damaged beyond repair. Sure, some of them do end up recovering, but, in the end, it's their minds that fail them. But you – you're the first person I've seen walk through these doors that I've felt hopeful about. There's something to save inside of you. You're worth saving."

From this exact moment, Tessa knew she was screwed. There was no world without Dr. Carmichael in it. He just became the most important person in her life. He was going to save her. She was worth saving.

———————

LUCY

He wasn't happy with my demands, but he's also not in any place to negotiate. He would probably go broke before he had to set foot back on these grounds. I asked for double the amount I owed Patty. It would be enough for me to give Patty more than I owed her and still allow myself a nice little Easter egg for safekeeping.

Lucy's sitting in her studio apartment in the pitch black. She's trained herself not to turn on any lights unless she absolutely has to. She can't afford to be lax with her utility bill. Or any bill, for that matter. Plus, she's gotten quite accustomed to the darkness. It suits her. The darkness has always been inside of her, coursing through her veins. If Lucy really thought about it, her entire life has been a dance of trying to keep the darkness bottled up inside of her. Up until now, she's done a pretty good job at it. But darkness is like a cancer that multiplies and spreads until it becomes uncontrollable. Lucy is keenly aware that the cancer is spreading. It's only a matter of time now.

Lucy dials Patty's number. To no surprise, she gets sent straight to voicemail.

Lucy clears her throat, "Honey, it's me. Great news! I've secured the money. I know you don't want to see me, but please let me give you the money. Please." The last please comes from the deepest part of Lucy's soul. If she can't make this right with Patty, she's unsure what will happen. She can't let her mind go there. She won't allow it.

She's fought this hard. She sure as hell isn't throwing in the towel now.

———————

AVA

Tommy and Ava sat in complete silence the entire boat ride back to the marina. It was all too similar to their previous boat ride back from the oyster farm.

As Tommy is maneuvering the boat back into the slip, Ava finally gets the courage to say something. She'd been wracking her brain the entire boat ride back, wondering what she did to make Tommy go cold.

"What, so that's it?" Ava asks.

Tommy looks confused, "I'm sorry?"

"You just decided to have sex with me and then rush me back home like I'm some whore you couldn't possibly be seen with?"

Tommy's mouth drops open. He's flabbergasted. "Wait, what? What are you talking about?"

"You've said nothing this entire boat ride back."

"Well, neither have you."

"Was I just some transaction to you? Another notch on the ole bedpost?"

Tommy closes the gap between them so he's an arm's reach away. He almost whispers his next sentence. "You're married." His eyes lower as he says it.

"Yes….and? You knew this. Like you said, you saw the wedding ring." Ava replies. There must be something she's missing, she thinks.

Tommy sits back down on one of the seat cushions. He looks like he just got punched in the gut. "I was worried that if we stayed and basked in it, you would start to regret it."

"What?" Now it's Ava's turn to be confused.

"You're married. And as much as I would like that

not to be the case, it's the facts. I would never ask you to leave him, and that absolutely rips me in two. Because what we just did there… that was something I've never experienced before. It was longing. It's as if my soul has been longing for this. For you. But this doesn't have a happy ending. There's only one person who gets hurt in all of this. Me. And as much as I want to say the pain will be worth it, I just don't know if that's true."

Ava sits down next to Tommy. Her heart has softened like melted ice cream on a summer day. This beautifully raw man deserves her honesty—her full honesty.

"Look, I don't know what the future holds. Yes, I am married. But I've also never missed someone before I even left them. That's how it feels with you. Like each moment is never enough. How could that even be possible when I haven't even known you a full week? I know these feelings have progressed rather quickly, but I'm not going to ignore the fact that you've lit something in me that I thought burned out long ago. You're right. It's not lust. I've had that before. This longing is so deep within me that it's hard to even understand if I've ever really longed for someone before you. I will never regret what we just did back there and I would really like to keep not regretting it if you'll allow it."

Ava was cautious not to make any promises. The truth is, she doesn't know what the future holds. As much as she wants more and more of this man sitting before her, she also recognizes that a life with Max Greenfield is not something to just throw away. She's worked too damn hard to build that life. After all, Tommy is merely a stranger. She knows virtually nothing about him. But that's the thing about strangers, isn't it? Pretty soon, you're left wondering how you ever lived a life that didn't include them in it. The only thing she is so resoundingly sure of in this moment is just how badly she wants to lead this beautiful stranger home – to her bedroom.

TESSA

Tessa is drooling like a houndog on her pillow. She's knee-deep in a dream. It's one of her favorites—the one where she's a little girl looking into a sand dollar mirror. A beautiful woman with golden blonde hair and bronzed skin is staring back at her in the same mirror. The mirror has sand dollars glued in each of the four corners. There's one sand dollar that's cracked in the bottom right corner. The once smooth edge of the sand dollar has turned jagged and sharp.

"You look beautiful, my little girly," the woman says. Tessa smiles proudly, as if her only job in the world is to sit there and look pretty.

"Not as pretty as you," little Tessa replies.

"One day, you're going to be old enough to understand that true beauty is on the inside. I want you to always remember that. Will you promise me you'll always remember that, Tessy?"

Little Tessa smiles and nods as the blonde engulfs her in a hug.

As she awakes, Tessa is hit with the reality of where she is. The grey stucco walls and the smell of Clorox comically taunt her. Did she really think she could dream away the reality of this awful place? She needs to see Dr. Carmichael and tell him about this dream. All these recurring dreams feel important. It's like these dreams are painting a picture of a reality that was once hers before the cruelness of life got in the way. Dr. Carmichael told her to lean into these dreams. They may be the key to unlocking her past. This is the first time in a while that Tessa has been sober enough to even remember these dreams. Maybe being stone-cold sober isn't so bad after all, Tessa thinks. Maybe, just maybe, she can finally start connecting the dots in the never-ending game of tic tac toe that seems to be her life.

AVA

It's been one full week in Chestertown. One whole week! If someone had told me I would be spending more than two days in this place, I surely would have never left London. While I didn't fully understand the reality that was waiting for me upon arrival, I somehow was expecting it. Lucy's slimy betrayal was unexpected, but meeting Tommy has turned out to be a very welcome surprise. In life, you take the good with the bad and hope the good outweighs the bad. Isn't that what my dad always used to tell me? Luckily, Lucy seems to be out of the picture. Since Lucy sent those pictures to Max I haven't seen or heard from her. It's probably because she knows there's nothing she can hang over my head anymore. She's done the very worst, and I'm still here standing in this town. Many things would drive me out of this town, but none of them start with Lucy and end with Gonazlez. I feel empowered now. It feels so good to take my power back.

Ava rolls over on the creeky couch and smiles at Tommy. He's sleeping lazily on his side. He looks so peaceful, almost like that upturned smirk is permanently tattooed on his lips. And those dimples. She can't get enough of those dimples.

After the boat ride, Tommy gladly accepted Ava's invitation to dinner. Dinner led to a couch cuddling session, which led to…you can guess the rest. And now Ava is admiring this man who has somehow made one week in Chestertown feel like not nearly enough time.

She's not exactly sure what the end game is for her. She'd be lying if she said she hadn't thought about Max since her night with Tommy at the fish fry festival. But the thoughts about Max have been more focused on the stark differences between him and Tommy. Where Max is loud and gregarious, Tommy is soft and sensual. Max likes to be the one to call the shots, while Tommy is more than okay letting Ava take the lead. Even the way they make love is so vastly different. Max is a one and done type of guy, always ready to get it over with. Tommy likes to take his time studying each part of Ava, as if he's preparing for a pop quiz. Ava once asked Max to slow it down in the bedroom. Max told her he was tired and just wanted to finish. These are not the words any woman wants to hear when being intimate with their partner. Max always used the excuse of being too tired to ward off any of Ava's advances. Ava finally stopped trying altogether. What was the point when your husband would reject you like you were some rotten fruit? Betsy always told Ava that if he wasn't getting it from her, he was getting it from someone else. That may be true in other marriages, but not in Ava's marriage. Ava's marriage was secure, wasn't it? Just because they hit a lull in their sex life doesn't automatically assume someone is cheating. However, it doesn't exactly ease Ava's mind either. Now that she thinks about it, Max has been working more than his regular hours. Ava just assumed he took on a new project requiring more of his attention. Had she been so complacent that she didn't see the signs? Now Ava was really getting herself down a rabbit hole.

Ava slowly stands up from the couch while Tommy is still fast asleep. She steps out onto the back deck and pulls her phone out of her sweatshirt pocket. She dials Max's number but gets sent straight to voicemail.

"It's me. We should talk."

_____

LUCY

Lucy rushes into Sunrise Cafe. She's completely out

of breath when she reaches the hostess stand. Before the
hostess can say anything, Lucy spots Patty sitting in the
corner booth. Lucy gives a frantic wave and beelines it
towards Patty.

"I'm so sorry, baby! We were short-staffed at work.
I had to clean double the rooms today. It was a mess. I
made it out of there as soon as I could!" Lucy says,
desperately trying to catch her breath.

She slides into the booth across from Patty.

Patty says nothing. She seems uninterested in her
mother's slew of excuses. Lucy is frazzled. It was difficult
enough getting Patty to agree to meet her here. Patty only
agreed to meet her mother if it was in a neutral spot. Patty
didn't want to risk having her mother over at her house
again.

"How are you dear?" Lucy asks, slowly easing into
the conversation.

"Mom," Patty says. She wants to say more but stops herself.

Lucy picks up on her daughter's curtness and pulls out an envelope from her purse. She slides it across the table. "Here you go. It's all of it and some change." Lucy winks at her daughter. She's trying to be cute and make light of this heavy situation. Patty is not at all amused.

The two of them look into each other's eyes as if they are willing the other person to blink first. Neither of them seem to want to back down from the challenge.

"Right. Well, I should get going." Patty finally breaks first. She grabs her purse but Lucy instinctively lunges across the table.

"Wait! Please, please don't go. We need to talk this out. This can't end like this!"

"End like what, mom?" Patty asks aggressively. "What? Did you think that you could just hand over the money you stole from us and we would just magically forget this ever happened?"

"Of course not. I know things need to be repaired. I also know it's not going to happen overnight."

"Or at all," Patty firmly corrects her.

Lucy physically recoils her body at her daughter's harsh words. Patty's eyes soften. She lets out a long, tired sigh.

"I don't want to hold onto this anymore. This hate. This resentment. It's not healthy for me." Tears well up in Patty's eyes. "It's not healthy for my family to see me like this. It's not who I am."

Lucy and Patty are both crying now. These are not the uncontrollable tears that come after a sudden tragic event. No, these tears flow slowly and steadily. These are the type of tears that hold the weight of years and years of pain.

"I don't know how we got this far off track, Mom," Patty continues.

"I don't either," Patty admits. She reaches her hand across the table and places it on top of Patty's. Patty lets her mother's hand stay there. "What I do know is I'm going to work at this every day to ensure we get back on track. I know I've been far from perfect. I know the trust has been broken. I'm not expecting you to throw open your arms and welcome me back. All I'm asking for you to do is crack the door open. And slowly, I hope I can show you just how serious I am."

Patty lets her mother's words hang in the air for a few moments. A waitress whirls by them with a freshly baked cinnamon roll. Patty clutches her rumbling stomach.

"Okay, Mom. Let's start with breakfast." Patty settles back down in the booth.

Lucy smiles. She knows she has a long road ahead of her, but she silently celebrates this pivotal moment. The door has been cracked open and Lucy will do absolutely anything she can to ensure it never closes again. Absolutely anything.

———————

TESSA

"Try to think back. Allow your mind to go there. You're in a safe place. You can let your mind go there." Doctor Carmichael instructs Tessa.

Tessa is laid out like a corpse on his office loveseat. It's a small loveseat, so her legs dangle off the side. Her eyes are firmly shut. You can see her eyeballs moving back and forth across her heavy eyelids.

"It's not working," Tessa whines.

"You're not trying. You're still too distracted. Go to the forest you told me about. Plant one foot firmly on the forest floor. You're amongst the trees now."

Tessa takes thirty rounds of very deep breaths. Her eyeball activity has slowed to almost a standstill.

"I hear a lot of noises," Tessa finally says.

"What kind of noises?" Doctor Carmichael asks.

Tessa furrows her brows, "They're calling my name."

"Who is there?"

"It's just me. I'm hiding behind a really large rock. I'm trying to be as quiet as possible."

"Why are you hiding?"

"I ran away. I ran away from the house."

"Your family house?"

"No. I'm behind the woods of the house—the house I was renting. I don't understand why I would be there. It doesn't make sense."

"Do you know why you ran away?"

"There was an argument. Between my Mom and I. My birth mom. I can see her as clear as day now. She has this remarkably large birthmark that covers half of her shoulder and part of her neck."

"What were you arguing about?"

"She told me she had to go away for a little while."

"Go where?"

"I don't know. She won't say. She promised me she'd be back. She promised she'd find me, and we will be together again soon. I'm crying."

"What else do you see?"

"I see my mom walking towards a boat that's docked near the boathouse. A man is standing next to me. I don't know who he is. He's tapping my head. For some reason, I can't make out his face. I'm getting really scared."

"Why are you scared?"

"He just seems scary. I'm turning around and running for the woods. I don't know what else to do but run. I want to run away from him. He's really scaring me."

Tessa's eyeballs are frantically darting left to right across her closed eyelids. Her heart rate has picked up.

"He won't leave me alone! Why is no one coming to help me? Help me!" Tessa screams, "Help me, please! Somebody!"

Doctor Carmichael taps Tessa on the shoulder, "I think that's enough for today. You can open your eyes. You did very well."

Tessa slowly opens her eyes and rearranges herself back to a sitting position on the loveseat. She grabs her chest as her heartbeat slows back down.

"I didn't like that at all."

"I know. Going back and revisiting the past can be scary, but it's really the only way to understand why this thing still holds you hostage."

"I feel like I'm almost there."

"Maybe. We really don't know until we get in there and see what we're dealing with." Dr. Carmichael says.

"Tessa, I wanted to follow up on our last conversation. I really do think it's in your best interest to check yourself out of here. This place will do nothing but chew you up and spit you back out. I've seen enough people sit on this very couch to know the longer you spend in here, the further you get from complete recovery, both mentally and physically. We've done some real work in just a few days. I can help you continue that work."

"I've been in enough of these places to know all of this." Tessa stubbornly replies.

Her visits to Dr. Carmichael's office have turned into daily, sometimes twice daily visits. At first, the visits were meant to steal her away from her boredom. After a while, she realized just how much she liked talking to him. He is the most interesting person she has met to date. Plus, she is determined to crack his cold, stiff exterior and get down into the meat and potatoes of his soul. These visits tend to skirt the perimeter of a Rubix cube she knows she shouldn't attempt to try. But she also can't think of any reasons not to try it. Now that she thinks about it, she's always been quite good at Rubix cubes.

"So get up and go," Dr. Carmichael interrupts her thoughts, "This is an at-will facility. No one here is holding you back."

"I told you this already," Tessa calmly replies. "I promised my brother I would try this time—really try. I can't let him down."

She means it, too. She's sure her heart would shatter right in two if she let her brother down yet again.

Dr. Carmichael scoots his chair closer to Tessa so they're painstakingly close without touching. "Will you at least think about it?"

Tessa nods. She would do almost anything this beautiful man asked of her. But Tommy – she must protect Tommy's heart. He's far too fragile, especially these days. He would understand, though, wouldn't he? Dr. Carmichael was resoundingly clear that he wouldn't pursue whatever this was between the two of them if Tessa remained a patient at the facility.

Tessa gets up from the loveseat and heads back toward her room. She's going to do something she hasn't done in a very long time. She's going to sit with her sober, unobstructed thoughts. She's going to think. For the first time in her life, someone seems to be giving her a way out from all this madness. Ava's accomplished more with Doctor Carmichael in just a few short days than she has in the years and years of therapy and psychotherapy she's undergone. All this time, she was trying to run away from her past, not knowing it might end up being the very thing that sets her free. How beautifully ironic, Tessa thinks.

———————

AVA

Ava woke Tommy up from the couch sometime after midnight and relocated him to the bedroom. The bed is a tiny queen, leaving little to no room for two people to sleep without touching. Ava more than prefers it that way.

Her brain refuses to shut off. She's not ready to fall back to sleep yet.

"Tell me about your childhood." Ava softly asks Tommy as she strokes through the knots in his blonde hair.

"Is this the part where you peel back the layers of my childhood, dissecting every nosebleed or time I pissed my pants?" Tommy jokes.

"No, but it can be. Sounds like you have some serious PTSD from pissing your pants. And by the sound of it, it may have happened more than once." Ava teases back.

"HA-HA! Very funny." Tommy clears his throat, "What specifically do you want to know?"

"What were you like as a kid?"

"Well, up until the age of six, I was pretty reckless and carefree. I wasn't afraid of anything. I felt pretty unstoppable in the world."

"And after six?" Ava presses.

"My little sister died just after my sixth birthday. She was three years old. Everything after six was really just a masterclass on life – the real life, not the one I was aimlessly floating through. My rose-colored glasses got shattered real quick."

"I'm so sorry."

Death has always freaked Ava out. She doesn't like to talk about it. She's lost all ability to even broach the topic of death. It's probably because immediately after her parent's accident, a slew of counselors told her ad nauseam not to be afraid of death. They told her that her parents were in a better place now. Ava was fairly confident that six

feet under was not the better place her parents had in mind.

"It's ok. Really," Tommy continues, "She was sick

for a while, so it wasn't a total surprise. It's been so many

years since it's happened. Most of the time, I forget about

it, but sometimes I –"

"You what?"

Tommy takes a breath, readying himself, "I don't

know how to describe it. Layla's death changed us all. Of

course it did. There was no scenario where it didn't

completely shatter our family. I knew that. But after her

death, my parents never let me out of their sight. No longer

could I go outside and play with the neighborhood kids or

go to the local field to play baseball with my friends. My

parents had a tight leash on me that was slowly choking

me. Suffocating me, really. I thought things would get

better once we adopted Tessa. I was hopeful she would take

the edge off of things a bit. Like, look, here's another tiny human you have. If something happens to me, you still have another one! But it doesn't work like that. My parents were just as suffocating with Tessa as they were with me. My mom even more so. She would dress Tessa in all these outfits that were a total copy and paste of what Layla used to wear. Tessa hated the outfits but Mom didn't care. Tessa had the same leash I had, if not a few inches shorter. As she got older, she started expressing her growing interest in finding out more about her birth parents. My mom and dad shut it down real quick. They were terrified her birth parents were going to realize where she lived and take her away from them. They couldn't lose a second child. And so that was our life. Looking out of windows, daydreaming about all the what ifs we would never get to experience."

"Wow," is all Ava can think to say. She knows all about the what if scenarios that rattle your brain just as much as she knows about looking out at life through a yellow stained glass window. Ava can't believe how similar Tommy's childhood is to hers.

"I know. Aren't you glad you asked me?" Tommy says mockingly. He's desperate to lighten up the conversation.

Ava takes Tommy's face in both her hands and delicately kisses the top of his forehead. She kisses his ear and the side of his cheek before finally landing on his lips. His lips are like a magnet to hers.

"I can't take away the pain of your childhood, as much as I want to."

"I know. I know," Tommy sighs.

"But I do know one thing that I can do to try and take your mind off of it..."

Ava reaches her hand down toward Tommy's nether regions. She leaves her hand strategically there.

Tommy's eyes go wide, "Oh yeah? What's that!?"

Before Ava can answer him, her phone lights up the dark room. She must have forgotten to turn it to silent before heading back to sleep.

Tommy is closer to the nightstand, so he rolls over to reach for Ava's phone. He momentarily freezes.

He hands Ava the phone, avoiding direct eye contact. This must be bad, Ava thinks.

Max's name is plastered across her phone.

"I think you should take this. It could be important." Tommy says before sliding out of bed and exiting the room.

Why is Max calling her at one in the morning? Ava quickly remembers it's six AM London time. The time difference has acted almost like a barrier for Ava, shielding her between her old and new life. Now, the time difference is a stark reminder that the old always catches up with the new. It's just a matter of time.

She takes the deepest breath she can muster and answers the call, "Hello?"

"Ava. I wasn't expecting you to answer. I was going to leave a voicemail."

"I've been trying to reach you, Max. Of course I'm going to answer. You're my husband." The last word, husband, comes out of Ava's mouth before she can take it back.

"What's going on? Are you ok?"

"Max, are you cheating on me?"

"Ava, what the fuck? Are you really asking me if I've been cheating on you when I have those pictures of you with that guy!?"

Max's tone has quickly changed from concern to anger.

"Please, just answer the question. I need to know. It's all out in the open now so there's no point in lying. Have you been unfaithful to me?"

There is a long pause as Ava's question hangs in the air. You can almost hear a pin drop from some three thousand miles away in London.

"Max. Please, just tell me," Ava begs.

"Fine. Yes, I've been unfaithful."

Ava buries her face in her hands. She bites down hard on her hand so she doesn't let out the audible scream that's sitting at the base of her throat. "For how long?"

"Ava, please. Let's not do this, ok?"

"I said, for how long, Max!"

"I don't know! It's hard to pinpoint. I guess it started right after our wedding when you got your first big promotion at work. But I ended it soon after that."

"Right after our wedding! You sure didn't waste any time, did you?"

"Don't do that, Ava. Don't you dare act all holier than thou after what you've been doing over there." Max threatens

"Why did you even marry me?"

Max sighs. This conversation was inevitable. It's been years in the making. Both Ava and Max have been skirting around this conversation for quite some time. "Because I wanted to be with you. Things changed when we got married, though. You became so obsessed with work. It's like I suddenly became an afterthought."

"Here you go again. Gaslighting me for having a successful career. I guess it's easy to do when your own career is complete shit, huh?"

"Some days you don't even kiss me goodbye before you go into work. You can make me the villain. I can take it. But what I won't take is you not owning up to your part in all this. You've been far from the perfect spouse."

"Oh, please! Don't blame me for all your mommy issues."

"You're acting like you have ground to stand on here. Are you forgetting about the pictures? Do you wanna know the most hurtful thing?"

Ava remains silent.

"It's not like you did this all out of retaliation," Max continues, "Because you didn't know anything about my unfaithfulness. No, you did this because you wanted to. You wanted to cheat on me. You wanted to know what it would feel like to be held softly in someone else's arms. So, it seems like we're not all that different after all, Ava McGready.

"How long did it go on?" Ava asks, ignoring Max's blatant dig at her. He's trying to rile her up, but she refuses to let her composure break.

Max says nothing. His silence speaks volumes.

Ava hangs up the phone. This time, she lets out an audible scream that comes from deep within her belly. She doesn't even try to muffle her anger because what's the point anymore? It's all out in the open, and Ava's pretty

sure that's not even the half of it.

WEEK TWO

LUCY

I didn't set out to get involved with Jeff McGready. I have a daughter, for God's sake. But eventually, the desperation creeps in and takes over. When you're that desperate, the lines of good and evil are utterly blurred. In fact, they're not even lines anymore. At least, not ones you can clearly distinguish. An opportunity is an opportunity. You best believe you will answer the call when an opportunity comes knocking. The money was just something I couldn't turn down. I know that sounds awful now, but you must understand how desperate I was. My daughter and I were sleeping in a tent behind the gas station. Patty is a type 2 diabetic and needed medicine. I would do anything to make sure she had her medicine. Anything. That included shipping innocent teenagers off to God knows where. I never asked where they were going. Part of the deal was I didn't want to know where they were going. I couldn't know.

I was convinced that somehow knowing would eat me alive from the inside out. Everything else was just about decompartmentalizing. I got really good at that. Little did I know this would all eat me alive, regardless. The demons can never be satiated, can they? They're always hungry for more.

AVA

The call from Max went exactly how I thought it would go until it didn't. He started the call acting all concerned for my well-being. After dodging my calls for two straight days, I didn't exactly have time for his fake sincerity. I wanted to get right to the point. He, of course, tried to throw it all right back in my face. How quickly he can switch when he's backed into a corner.

Admittedly, I can't say I expected Max to welcome me back with open arms. Not that I would have necessarily wanted him to. For the last few days, Tommy and I have spent virtually every waking minute together. No, Max asking me to hop on the first jet out of here and back into his arms would have complicated things more than I can begin to comprehend. What I did not prepare myself for was the bombshell of all bombshells, which was Max confirming that he not only had an affair but that he was still having an affair.

Of course, I have no ground to stand on. Aren't I doing exactly the same thing he is doing? Sure, it may not be the exact same, but a spade is a spade any way you look at it. Even I can't deny that. So yes, while I didn't expect Max to have it in him to cheat, I guess I've always intuitively known that a life with Max Greenfield would never be permanent. My childhood was the biggest proof of that point. I'd been tossed around from foster home to foster home, praying something would stick. Praying that a family would think I'm lovely (or tolerable) enough to keep me. But as I've said before, you learn to take the good with the bad in life. The biggest piece de resistance, though, was the moment I found out that Max had shut off our joint bank account. The one I'd worked so hard to build up like it was one of those drip castles you build at the beach. Poof. Gone.

I was the one who pleaded with Max to keep our bank accounts separate. I didn't want to rely on another man, especially when I'd worked so hard to build up my career and finally make partner at the firm. My job, the one that eagerly awaits me back home in London, means everything to me. It's been a little over a week since I've been at work and people are starting to grow uneasy. Betsy has already left me three voicemails that I have no intent on listening to. It's as if taking off more than a week for 'vacation' is a crime. For me, I guess it is. At the firm, I silently judged those who would jet off on their week(s) long European vacations. If I really think about it, I've never taken more than three days off since starting at

Archer Architects. It was for my "mini-moon". Max

wanted to go away for a long weekend to sip champagne in

the English countryside. He assured me we would take a

proper honeymoon once things settled down. The problem

was that things never settled down, did they? I now wonder

if he wanted to return to London so quickly so that he could

see his mistress. Right after our wedding was when it all

started, isn't that what Max had said? I wonder what she

looks like. Is she prettier than me? She sure as hell isn't

smarter than me. Or maybe she is. After all, how could I

have gone all these years not knowing? How could I have

not seen the signs?

    Max assured me that having a joint bank account

would save us a lot of headaches in the future. "It's easier

this way," he told me countless times, "especially when our

future children would be in the picture." Our future

children. How often had we droned on and on about our

'future children', as if they were some imaginary mountain peak we had yet to summit? He also assured me that what's his is mine and vice versa (although, if we're being honest, he had quite a significant amount more than I did sitting in that joint account). His trust fund inheritance was just starting to kick in when I met him. I agreed because – well, love. I agreed because that tiny gesture of someone wanting to be linked up with me meant more than I could articulate. All my life, no one ever desired to be linked up with me. But here was Max, wanting to link up with me. How could I not say yes? So here I am now. Dumb, broke, and very, very desperate. I'm just like the heroin in all the novels we've read about too many damn times. So now it's never been more important to call the developer and get him out to survey the property this week. This plot of land that holds such a dichotomy in my heart will now be my saving grace, just when I needed it the most. In the eleventh hour, as they say. Eleven has always been my favorite number.

TESSA

The plan is to leave on Thursday. I promised Tommy a month, and I had every intention of keeping that promise. I really did. But then I met Doctor Carmichael. Alex Carmichael. He told me to call him by his first name. He said when I called him Doctor, it felt wrong. He said calling him by his professional name would make what we were doing wrong. I think what we're doing is anything but wrong. It all just feels SO right. I plan to live at Alex's apartment for a few weeks as I transition back into the real world. Professionally, he wants to keep a close eye on me. Personally, I think he wants to see me with my clothes off. But I'm not going to let that happen. I've given myself up so easily to so many men. I know better now. As much as I'd love to have my lips on his, I'm playing the long game here. Alex is different. I just know it. I feel it in my bones. I know Tommy will be beyond pissed, but I'm hopeful he will

come around. He will see I never needed a facility to set me

straight. All it took was for one person to crack me wide

open and let all the sunlight filter in. If that isn't enough to

set someone straight, I don't know what is. After my

two-week transition, I plan to use the money from the house

to rent a modest one-bedroom apartment on the East side of

town. I will leave my new apartment sparkling clean.

Orderly. Alex says I need order. I need structure in my life

and a consistent and easily repeatable routine. Maybe I'll

pick up yoga. I've always been quite flexible…

AVA

"Please don't be like this." Ava is pacing back and forth as Tommy sits at the kitchen table.

It's very early in the morning, but neither Ava nor Tommy slept a wink. Tommy came rushing into the bedroom with a bat as soon as Ava ended the call with Max. She screamed so loud he thought there was an intruder. After he understood Ava was just having a mental break, he sat down next to Ava and held her hand. Ava let it all out. She told Tommy everything. He deserved to know the truth and not some muddled version of it. She wasn't exactly sure how Tommy would react. Then again, she wasn't really sure how even she would react to the news. Ava still isn't really sure.

"I just think you need some time to think about things," Tommy says.

"Think about what?! My husband cheated on me! My husband is still cheating on me! There's nothing more to think about," Ava cries out.

"This was almost ten years of your life, Ava."

Ten years. That number causes a pang in the side of

Ava's gut that resembles a burst appendix. Ava would know

the feeling. When she was six, she woke her dad up in the

middle of the night with an awful scream. She was lying in

the middle of the bathroom, crumbled up into a ball. She

was scared to move, fearful that any movement would

trigger a new wave of pain down her entire right abdomen.

Her dad ran into the bathroom, took one look at Ava, and

scooped her up off the floor and into his old pickup truck.

On the way to the hospital, Ava kept wondering where the

hell her mother was. All she wanted right then in that

moment was her mother.

Ten years. June fifth would mark ten years of Ava's

marriage to Max. Ten years since Max rescued Ava from

the desperation that was getting ready to close in on her.

Ten years of a safe and stable life on the outskirts of

London proper. Ten years of someone choosing to link up

with Ava. And choosing that every single day for some

3652 odd days. Ten years of mostly blissful contentment.

But what Ava has realized this past week is that

contentment does not necessarily equal happiness. Ava is

starting to realize that contentment can get easily

misconstrued as happiness. Sure, there were happy

moments and even happy years when Ava truly felt

unstoppable. But she was mostly just content when she

really thought about it. Content that she was far, far away

from Chestertown and all its ugliness. Content that she

would never have to worry again about saving on

electricity. Content that her credit card would never again

get declined at the local bodega. Content in knowing that

she finally found a man who would stay.

"Anything can happen. He can decide this was all a

big mistake and whisk you back to London." Tommy

replies, bringing Ava back to the present.

"He cheated on me, Tommy," Ava replies,

immediately regretting those words as soon as they're out

of her mouth. Tommy and Ava blush because they know

those words are like the pot calling the kettle black.

"I just think a few days will do you some good.

Alone. To clear your head and think this through. It will

only muddy the waters if I'm here with you."

"But I want you here," Ava pleads. In this moment,

she looks and sounds like she's seven years old again. She's

reaching out and clinging to anything she can hold onto. In

the months after her parents' death, Ava would beg and

plead, asking God to bring her parents back. She promised

God she would go to church every day and do all her

chores if he brought her parents back. While her family

wasn't the most religious type, she always believed in a

higher power that was looking down on her. Everything

after the accident changed Ava's view on that. While she

wasn't necessarily an atheist, she couldn't subscribe to the

whole idea of there being a 'righteous God.' How could he

be righteous if he let something like that happen to her

parents? After the accident, she quickly realized only one thing to be true: No one is coming to save you. It's you against you.

As if sensing Ava's growing apprehension, Tommy walks toward Ava and envelopes her in a big bear hug.

"Ava, I want all of you." Tommy lifts Ava's head so he can look into her deep ocean-blue eyes, "I don't want half of you or even two-thirds of you. I want every little piece of you. But how can I truly know if I'm getting all of you if your mind is elsewhere?" Tommy taps Ava's head to accentuate this point. "I'll be here for you when you decide, even if it's just taking you to the airport so you can fly back to London and back to your old life. I'll still be here for you. I'm not going anywhere. But you owe it to yourself to sit with this and not run from it. Sit with this all and see where it lands. You owe yourself that much."

Ava attempts to respond, but deep down she knows Tommy's right. She knows every point he made is valid.

Ava really does need to sit with this. She also knows that

that was Tommy's nice way of saying he doesn't want to be

her rebound. Ava can't blame him. She would feel the same

way if roles were reversed. As much as she hates to admit

it, Ava knows she needs to make sure she's not just running

to the next best thing like she's been so keen to do all her

life.

So now Ava is sitting with it all. She's looking at it

square in the eye. She's shaking hands with it. She's asking

it what it wants for breakfast because she's absolutely

ravenous.

TESSA

Tommy dropped in for a surprise visit this morning.

He was in an absolute pissed-off mood. Before he even

opened his mouth, I could tell something was off. His body

language was very, very off. I tried to ask him what was up, but he just waved me off. He wanted to talk about how I was doing in here and what kind of progress I've been making. I wasn't going to tell him about Doctor Carmichael (I mean, Alex) and our plan, especially after seeing him in such a piss-poor mood, but he kind of forced it out of me. He was irate. Actually, irate would be the understatement of the year. I was scared shitless. I was scared I wouldn't be able to calm him down. I was terrified when Tommy threatened to expose Alex and report him to the facility and the Maryland Board of Physicians. Alex would probably lose his license and undoubtedly never talk to me again. I couldn't let that happen. So, I did something I'm not proud of but I didn't see any other option. I told Tommy I would kill myself if he exposed Alex. I know it's awful and it felt so disgusting to say it out loud, but I couldn't lose Alex. He was the one thing that finally felt worth living for.

"I don't know anything about you." Tessa says. She's back on the loveseat in Doctor Carmichael's office.

Tessa told Doctor Carmichael all about Tommy's visit and what she said to him.

"Even more reason why you shouldn't have said those things." Doctor Carmichael responds calmly.

"I don't agree," Tessa snaps back.

Doctor Carmichael takes a drawn-out breath. "Tessa, we've talked about this. These extreme reactions are just another cry for help — a help you're so desperately searching for in external factors. To get the real help you need, you must go within. It's the only way. You know this."

"And if I were to go within, what exactly would I find that I haven't already found?" Tessa asks. It's a question that seems innocent, like something a five-year-old would ask. But Tessa is smart enough to know the answer is far from innocent.

"It depends," Doctor Carmichael responds. He remains patient yet steadfast.

"On what?"

"On many things, but mostly just how deep you're willing to go. Your body has a self-soothing mechanism designed to help you survive even the most traumatic events."

"I would say my life has been pretty traumatic, wouldn't you?"

"It has been. But I would also argue being given up for adoption is not an uncommon trauma. Children who have been given up for adoption and felt these very same feelings of abandonment have recovered. Many have gone on to live quite successful lives. There's something else in there." he points to Tessa's heart, "Something you have yet to uncover. Something that's been holding you back. The brain is a powerful organ that can hold a tremendous amount of suppressed information. Your job is to uncover that information, as hard as it may be."

"Sounds very hard."

"Oh, it's beyond tough. It will take a lot of work, silence, stillness, and uncomfortable conversations with yourself."

"And if I find it? Then what do I do?"

Doctor Carmichael smiles, "Then you set it free."

LUCY

I can't believe I'm back in this mess. I've tried so hard to run as far away from it as I could. And yet, here it is again being thrust in my face. Here I am again, crouched behind this damn bush. Watching her and the developer scour every inch of this property, including the boat house. I had to stifle my scream as they went around the perimeter of the boat house and walked along the sunflower garden. I planted that garden all those years ago as a remembrance to them. A way to honor them. I would have never gotten involved with it all if I had ever thought lives would be lost. Never. We got in too deep—way, way too deep.

Lucy thinks back to the first day she met Jeff McGready. She was working at Lucile's restaurant, one of the only restaurants in town that was open past ten P.M. Given her typical clientele at this time of night, she was preparing herself for a long night ahead. While she wasn't proud of the fact that she would sometimes entertain the customers after hours at the cheap motel down the street, she needed the money. She was beyond broke. She was behind in rent at the last apartment in town that would accept her application. When you've been evicted more than a handful of times, you aren't exactly the prime candidate in a landlord's eye. Lucy knew that if she were evicted one more time, there would be no other place for her to turn besides living back on the streets. She couldn't do that to Patty again. Patty had finally gotten into a routine and was thriving at school. So when Jeff McGready ordered a soda water and tipped Lucy two hundred dollars, she knew Jeff might be her temporary solution. Lucy expected Jeff to hang around until Lucy clocked out for the

night, but instead, he downed his soda water and slipped

her a note. The note simply said: *I have a job for you that*

doesn't require taking your top off. Meet me at 1211 Happy

Hollow Road at 4 A.M. tomorrow morning. Lucy was

beyond confused. This man was not looking for sexual

favors. He wasn't even looking to see her tonight. While

she was fairly confident there was a fifty-fifty chance

meeting Jeff alone at four AM would result in her making

the Chestertown obituary, she didn't have any other choice.

Money talks and this money was quite the chatterbox.

AVA

Ava waves goodbye to the man from Neff

Developers. She should be thrilled at the number looking

back at her on the piece of paper she's holding. The man

assured Ava this property was worth well over seven

million dollars. A week ago, she would have been ecstatic

about this number. Given the recent developments over the

past few days, she should be more than ecstatic with this

number. With this money, she can maintain the cushiony

lifestyle she's grown accustomed to and not need Max or

any man for that matter. But here she stands on this land,

struggling to catch her breath. This land that she's only

really just met. This land that holds the key to her past and,

coincidentally, her future. Her very rich future. This land

feels sacred to her, but for reasons she can't explain. It's as

if this land is scattered with millions of little Matryoshka

dolls that open up to reveal another hidden key. The

problem is that Ava is unsure which key goes where and

which key she should throw away for good.

Ava sighs. She climbs up the steps to the back deck

and takes a seat on one of the wooden rocking chairs. She

pulls out her phone from her back pocket and dials the only

person she wants to talk to right now. Betsy picks up on the third ring.

"Ava! Holy shit! It's you. You had me so worried. I've been trying to call you to tell you we got the bid! We just got the signed contract back. It's official! We're going to be redesigning the London tube! The London fucking tube! We need to celebrate! Wait, when are you coming back? I heard you needed a few more days away. Ava, I need to see you! We need to celebrate!" Betsy says, not taking a single breath between sentences.

"I know, Bets. I'm so sorry. It's all just been…." Ava's voice is shaking, "A mess." The last two words come out in a heaping sob. Ava is hunched over in the rocking chair, coming completely undone.

After about a half hour of Ava telling Betsy everything, she finally pauses. It feels so good to tell her best friend everything. She's not just inviting Betsy to peek behind the curtain; she's inviting her to grab her popcorn and watch the entire show.

"Well, shit. You really have been busy." Betsy says. "So the celebratory dinner tab will be on you, right?"

Ava ignores her friend's attempt to lighten the mood, "I don't even know if there's a life for me in London anymore."

"Don't say that! Of course there is! Even without Max, you still have so many friends here who would welcome you back with open arms!"

Ava doesn't know if that's the truth. In reality, most of her friends in London are an extension of Max. They were his friends first, and Ava is pretty sure none of them have genuinely accepted her. They've just tolerated her, almost as a favor to Max. Betsy is Ava's only friend who has no affiliation to Max.

"Almost ten years with Max feels like something I shouldn't just throw away. I need to fight for this. Fight for us. Right?"

"I can't answer that for you," Betsy replies. "What I can tell you is that some people spend an entire lifetime with someone they barely know. Sure, they know their favorite snack or ideal sleeping temperature, but they don't really know them. And then, sometimes, you find that rare person you want to spend a lifetime getting to know. And a lifetime is still not enough. It's up to you to decide which lifetime you want to fight for."

Ava smiles to herself. Besty has described her situation perfectly. She's always had this uncanny ability to read between the lines with people. It's truly a gift.

"I just don't know what to do. I need someone to tell me what to do."

"No. No, you don't. It's pretty simple, really."

"What?" Ava asks, confused. Everything about her situation seems anything but simple.

"Who was the first person you wanted to call after the developer left?"

"You, duh." Ava jokes.

"Obviously. But that's not what I meant! You know what I meant."

Ava knows exactly what Betsy meant. Just like she knows exactly what the answer is. It's staring at her right in the face. As clear as day.

———————

LUCY

Pulling onto 1211 Happy Hollow Road at four in the morning had to be one of the dumbest moves I've made. How many times had I preached to Patty about the importance of stranger danger? I felt like a sitting duck who swam very far from help. Ultimately, I got out of the car and followed Jeff McGready to the dark boathouse because I thought the reward outweighed the risk. Either I take this illusive job this man is presenting to me, or he kills

me and Patty gets my life insurance money; money that will

surely be enough to cover her until college. Patty was

determined to be the first member of the Gonzalez family to

graduate college. I needed to get Patty to college from this

side of the grave or the other. The offer seemed fake at first.

I had a hard time comprehending what Jeff was presenting

to me. He carefully laid out the complex and connected

network within the 'transportation industry' that he would

like me to become a part of. When I asked Jeff what we

would be transporting, he simply shrugged and said

humans. I asked him to repeat his answer two more times. I

was not understanding. Once it finally clicked, I politely

declined and thanked him for his time. I didn't want to piss

off a man who may have thoughts of killing me. Within

seconds, he produced a huge wad of cash from his back

pocket. He told me he was holding five thousand dollars.

Five thousand dollars was the amount I would get paid for

each 'drop off.' Five thousand dollars would pay for all the missed rent I owed and still give me enough change to buy Patty something other than deli meat for lunch. The details of the job were obscure. Jeff told me it was designed that way. Follow orders, ask no questions and complete the job. Those were the three rules. I knew I was making a decision I could never come back from. I knew what saying yes to the job meant. What I did not know was the extent of just how much the needle on my moral compass kept changing until it finally broke completely off.

Lucy smiles as she opens her arms wide and waits for her granddaughter to scoot down the slide.

Elisa slides into Lucy's arms and they both squeal with delight.

It's the perfect sunny fall afternoon. Lucy is beyond grateful for some supervised time with her granddaughter.

Elisa runs over to the seesaw and climbs aboard.

Lucy takes a seat next to Patty on the bench. They watch as

Elisa plays with another girl on the seesaw.

"She really is so sweet. She has your temperament."

Lucy says.

"I'm not too sure. I think I have your fiery streak."

Patty replies.

"Me? No!" Lucy jokes as she grabs her chest in

disbelief, "Not me!"

Patty and Lucy both let out a simultaneous laugh.

"This is nice," Lucy says, "I've missed this."

"I have too," Patty motions to her daughter, "We

have too."

"I would love to have an afternoon with her, just the

two of us. It's been so long since we've had some

one-on-one time." Lucy presses.

"Mom, we talked about this," Patty replies calmly,

"Baby steps. I still don't feel comfortable with that yet. It's going to take time."

Lucy gives an understanding nod, but a sadness has crept in behind her tired yes. "Yes, of course. I know."

Lucy and Patty sit silently for a few more moments as they watch Elisa being spun around by the other little girl. They both fall to the ground in a fit of laughter. It's the definition of carefree.

"So, do I want to know where you got the money?" Patty finally asks.

"Do you really need to know?" Lucy replies. She's been waiting for this moment. The moment when Patty's suspicion would begin to creep in.

Patty lets this question hang in the air momentarily, visibly debating this. Finally, she replies, "No. No, I guess I don't."

Lucy smiles, relieved at this answer. Lucy would have never told the truth anyway. She could never tell Patty she gave her soiled money. She could never admit that to her because that would mean she would never get moments like this again. Lucy wouldn't risk that. Not when she finally has her family back.

TESSA

Tessa is steeping the tea in her mug as she walks around Alex's kitchen. She's in her pajamas and her blonde hair is pushed high into a ponytail. It's far too early for anyone to be up.

Tessa takes a seat at the big farm table. She grabs her notebook and pen and stares down at a blank page.

"Writer's block?" Alex asks from behind her.

Tessa whips around, "Shit! You scared me!"

"Sorry, you just look so cute when you're concentrating. Your brow was so furrowed." Alex says. He kisses the top of her head.

It's been a few days since Tessa temporarily moved in with Alex. Tessa has emphasized the word temporary any chance she gets. She wants Alex to know she's not some freeloader. They both agreed it's important for her to build her own life, separate from him. The transition couldn't have been smoother. Tessa is finding out just how fond she is of her new morning routine. She used to dread mornings because that usually meant she would be greeted by a throbbing headache and a mouth as dry as the Sahara. She thought she would hate spending ten minutes a day writing down her thoughts, but it's proven to be quite soothing. She's even switched from coffee to tea. Hell really has frozen over.

"I was just thinking how I really don't like this journal. It doesn't inspire me. I had the most beautiful blue journal covered with big peacock feathers back at the old house," Tessa says, sipping her tea. "I'm going to stop by this week to get it. I would put it behind the china cabinet for safekeeping. I bet it's still there."

Alex spins Ava around in her chair and gives her a long, slow kiss. "Sounds beautiful. Just like you."

Tessa pushes him away, "Get out of here! You're messing up my routine!"

Alex slowly moonwalks out of the kitchen. Tessa smiles. Everything just feels so right. Since arriving at Alex's house, the pieces seem to have fallen into place. Tessa has remained firm in her no sleeping together boundary. So far, they've just kissed. And while both Tessa and Alex are tempted to do much more, they both know they're playing chess, not checkers. For once, Tessa has found someone playing the same game as her. It's the same game with the same rules. Checkmate.

AVA

Ava's sitting in Tommy's Boston Whaler with two coffee tumblers in hand. She's lost in thought as she watches the sun slowly start to peek above the Chesapeake Bay. Every single sunrise reminds her of her dad. He used to count the seconds until the sun finally rose from its sleeping spot. It's as if they were at Times Square on New Year's Eve, waiting for the ball to drop. It was a routine she cherished with her whole heart. It was their thing.

Ava spots Tommy's car pulling into the marina parking lot. She's unsure how he will react when he sees her, but she needs to see him. It's been two long days of Ava sitting with her unobstructed thoughts.

Ava stands just as Tommy approaches the Whaler. Steam is escaping from the tumblers and the smell of freshly brewed coffee wafts into the salty brine air.

"Ava?" Tommy asks. "What are you doing here?"

Ava smiles but says nothing. She waves him onto the boat and pats the seat next to her. Tommy is a bit apprehensive, but he climbs aboard and sits. Ava lowers

herself next to him so their thighs are almost touching.

Almost.

"I know you said I needed time to think things over,

and I wanted to let you know I've thought things over. So

before I begin, I just want you to know this wasn't some

snap decision. This was carefully thought through. Thank

you for being patient with me. Thank you for encouraging

me to take all the time I needed."

"Of course," Tommy says, still looking quite

apprehensive.

"My life in London isn't perfect, but it's pretty

damn near close. I have carefully created a life that just

makes sense. I live in a safe neighborhood, just far enough

away from the city but close enough to make my commute

to work bearable. I have a job I adore, and I'm pretty good

at it too. I just found out we won our bid to redesign the

London tube. It's the biggest bid ever won at the firm and

would keep me busy for the next three years. The commission I'll get off the project doesn't hurt, either. My marriage to Max is repairable, even given the recent developments. He's not a bad guy. He just gets a bit lost at times. And he really does treat me well —"

"Ava, it's ok," Tommy says, putting up his hand to stop her, "Really, you don't need to go any further. I get it."

Ava puts her hand on Tommy's thigh, "Wait. I'm not done." Ava steadies herself. She takes a deep breath before continuing, "I've spent my whole life chasing stability. Chasing the knowns. It makes sense, given my entire childhood was one big cluster fuck of unknowns. I learned to settle for a predictable life. A mundane life." Ava turns her body even more so that she has a clear shot of Max's face and his hazel green eyes, "But I don't want that life anymore. It never really was the life I was meant to live. It was only a life I stumbled upon while running from the life I was destined for. I want all the unknowns. You see, I'm not scared of them anymore. In fact, I'm welcoming them in with open arms. I want spontaneous six AM oyster shucking runs. I want back porch nights on two very broken rocking chairs. I want slow afternoons just as much as I want fish fry on Friday nights. I want all of these unknowns, and I think I want all of them with you. For however long that should be. I'm not saying we should get married tomorrow or even that we should date. I'm even okay if you just want to be friends. But what I do know is that I crave you in my life. I need you in my life. In whatever capacity that is. In whatever capacity you'll allow."

Tommy looks out over the water. The sun has fully risen and is casting amber hues over the marina. He looks over at Ava. She's glowing in the morning sun.

Tommy starts laughing. "I could never be just friends with you," Tommy grabs Ava's face in his hands, "I can be a lot of things with you, but I can never be just friends with you." Tommy leans in and gives Ava a soft kiss before pulling away.

They both are looking at each other, basking in the sunlight.

"So let's be more than friends," Ava says, her eyes still half closed from that last kiss.

"So let's be more than friends."

———————

LUCY

Lucy places a sunflower over a large patch of dirt. Jeff Mcgready is standing beside Lucy, a shovel in his left hand.

"This is all your fault," Lucy whispers.

"My fault? How dare you say that. You fucked up. You let her die. That was not my job." Jeff fires back.

"I want out. I can't do this. There has to be a way out."

"You can't get out. There is no out in any of this. Don't you understand?"

"There has to be an out. I can't do this. This was not a part of the deal. This is not who I am! I'm a mother!" Lucy cries out. She's hysterical now.

Jeff places his hand around Lucy's mouth, "Shut up before someone hears you!"

Lucy takes a few deep breaths to steady herself.

"I'll give you back all the money. I don't know how, but I'll give it all back to you. Please. Please just let me get out of this. I never wanted any of this!"

Jeff grabs Lucy's shoulders, "You think I wanted this! Look, there is no out – there is no exit plan. Follow orders, ask no questions, and complete the job. You know the rules."

Lucy's eyes shoot open. Her entire mattress is wet from sweat. The clock reads one in the morning. She gets up and stumbles over to the kitchen to put a tea kettle on the stove. There's no way she's going back to sleep now. She knows what's waiting for her on the other side of that dream.

TESSA

"I really don't want to go there," Tessa says to Doctor Carmichael. She's lying on the carpeted bedroom floor in Alex's apartment.

"You don't have to go there if you don't want to." Doctor Carmichael assures her.

"But I know I need to go there. If I want to be free of it I need to force myself to go there."

Doctor Carmichael says nothing. He wants Tessa to get there on her own.

Tessa closes her eyes. After about ten minutes of silence, she begins speaking again.

"My mom - my adopted mom. She was always yelling at me for something. But this time it's different. It's like her whole demeanor has changed."

"How so?" Doctor Carmichael probes.

"She's not just mad at me; she's disgusted with me. The look in her eyes. She's shaking me and telling me to stop crying. I'm yelling at her, saying she's not my mom. I'm telling her my real mom is coming back – that she'll be back any day now. It must be early on if I still believed that."

"You think your mom is coming back?"

"Yeah, I guess I do. I just keep yelling at my adopted mother that she's not my real mom. It's getting worse and worse. She slaps me. She's mad I can't be more like Layla. She's telling me how stupid I am compared to Layla."

"Do you believe it?"

"Yes."

_____

LUCY

This is the very last thing I wanted to do. This is, all things considered, the last case scenario. A scenario I tried so hard to avoid since Ava Greenfield touched down back in Chestertown a little over a week ago. I tried to scare her off, but she just kept coming back for more. I should have known trying to run her off the road in that truck would be a waste of time. But Jeff was clear. I had to do whatever was necessary to make this all go away. He gave me the money with the expectation that I would make this all go away. There are no takebacks with Jeff McGready. And you sure as shit wouldn't dare to pull a fast one over him. He would go after Patty and Elisa. It's the threat he's hung over me since the first day I got involved with him. It's a threat he reiterated about a dozen times on that fateful night. When Jeff called an emergency meeting, I knew it wouldn't be good. I was preparing myself for the worst, not knowing that the worst would still be better than what he

was asking me to do. Asking is putting it nicely. Again, he

reminded me that one misstep or slip of the tongue and

Patty and Elisa would pay the price. So what other choice

did I have? I had to fight to muffle the scream in my throat

as he carefully laid out his plan. He was going to take a

drive and hit the tree just right. I had to be at the meeting

spot to collect Ava. He wanted me to get her out of there as

fast as possible. I begged and pleaded with him. There had

to be another way. He told me his decision was final. He

told me this was the only way – she wasn't going to let it

go…so, ultimately, she had to go.

AVA

As Ava approaches the front gates of the property,
her heart sinks. Seeing Lucy's Honda sends a wave of chills
down her spine. The morning coffee she just enjoyed with

Max threatens to regurgitate itself back up all over her rental car.

Ava parks the car and places her shaking hands on the steering wheel. She needs to steady herself. She will not let Lucy intimidate her. Not this time. She's already done the worst possible thing to Ava. What else could possibly be left? The last couple of days have changed her. Ava feels stronger and more sure of herself. She's found her footing in this town. She's faced the worst head-on and still managed to come up swinging. Bring it on, Lucy fucking Gonalez. Bring it on.

Ava exits her car just as Lucy does the same. It's almost like they're two paid actors dropped into a Western standoff scene.

"You need to leave," Ava says calmly yet clearly.

Lucy continues the stare down yet says nothing.

269

"You need to leave," Ava repeats herself. "Or I'm sure the police will be more than happy to make you leave."

"Oh, that won't be necessary to involve the police." Lucy finally says.

"Oh? And why is that?" Ava asks. She crosses her arms, willing herself to stand as straight as her body will allow.

"Because you're going to listen to what I have to say. And if you want to call the police after that, be my guest." Lucy says, "But I'm fairly positive you won't want to do that after what I have to say."

Everything inside Ava's brain is screaming for her to run. To get back into the rental car and gun it out of here. Instead, she takes a step forward. She will face this.

"You know, I really do have a soft spot in my heart for you," Lucy continues without permission, "You're a fighter. You kind of remind me of myself. We've both had to scratch and claw to earn what is ours our entire life. I can relate to that more than you know. But your downfall has always been your blind determination. You just don't know when to throw in the towel. The difference between a good fighter and a great fighter is that a great fighter knows when to throw in the towel. They know when they've been cornered and their time is up. They know when to tap out. I tried to give you every out I could think of, but you just won't go away. You keep coming back for more. It's like you're hungry for more. I really thought the pictures of you with that man would drive home the point of just how serious I am. But here you are, still standing on this property."

"I feel sorry for you," Ava interrupts, "I do. I've actually always felt sorry for you. Being the kind of person who threatens and attacks people, especially at their weakest moments, can't be easy. It must get tiring after a while. They say the best way to defeat a bully is to hold up a mirror to them. To make them look themselves square in the eyes. And then let them know it's okay to let that bully go. You've always carried this sadness inside of you that you never seemed like you could shake. You don't have to be a prisoner anymore. You can let that bully go. As a fellow fighter, I'm giving you an out. I'm giving you the option to throw in the towel. To get back in your car and drive away. And get as far away from the bully as you can."

Lucy lets out a laugh. It's bone-chilling. It's an unsettled laugh that even Lucy herself seems to be afraid of. The look on Ava's face indicates she surely is.

"What I didn't tell you about a great fighter is that they will never throw in the towel on a fight they know they can win. They will give it their absolute all in a fight where the odds are stacked in their favor."

"And you think the odds are stacked in your favor? I'm no statistics major, but trespassing on private property doesn't really seem like a probable outcome for you. Trying to run over someone with a truck also doesn't sound like a probable outcome for you."

There it is, that laugh again. It's one that comes from deep within Lucy's belly.

"What can I say? People love an underdog." Lucy smirks.

"I'm not giving you a cent," Ava retorts back. "When you came here last time I was going to give you money, and not just because I wanted those pictures erased. Unbeknownst to you, you actually did me a favor. So, I want to thank you. You helped me stop running. You helped me see that running was actually only bringing me right back to the very thing I was running from. I wanted to give you the money because you seemed like you really needed it. I was hopeful you could use the money to do something good with your life. To help yourself or your family. But what I realize now, as you stand here with that dirty smirk on your face, is that you will never change. You won't change because you can't. It's not in your DNA. You will always be a bully simply because some people are just born evil. They can't help it. So, the money you came for has come and gone, just like you. You've come. Now you really should be going."

Lucy looks at Ava with softened eyes. Ava seems to have struck a nerve. For a moment, Ava thinks she may have finally gotten through to Lucy. The moment quickly fades as Lucy regains her composure. The darkness in her eyes is back like it never left.

"I told you, I didn't come here for money. It wasn't about the money then, and it definitely isn't about the money now," Lucy says. "You're not understanding. You know, for as smart and successful as you are, sometimes you're just plain dumb."

"As dumb as a fighter not knowing when to throw in the towel?" Ava asks. "Because that's what you are right now. Throw in the towel, Lucy. This is over."

"Oh, this is far from over Ava." Lucy fires back. "We've only just begun, which brings me to the point of why I'm here today. You can't sell this property."

Ava sighs, "I told you this already. You're not getting any money. You feel like you're owed money for this property for reasons I can't understand. My name is on the will, not yours. This is my property and you're not getting a dime. How much clearer do I have to be?"

"I don't want to do this."

"Do what? Send incriminating pictures to my husband? Well, newsflash, you already went there! There's nothing left to hang over me. It's all been done. I'm still standing. On MY property. Demanding, not asking, that you leave. Your time is up."

Ava walks past Lucy and pushes open the gates to the house with gumption.

"Paul Summers." Lucy spits out, almost like it's a foul word.

Two words. Those two words were all it took to send Ava's orbit completely crashing down.

Ava once read about a woman who was kidnapped from the age of six to eight years old. Luckily, she was reunited with her family, and she grew up to have absolutely no recollection of the time she was held captive. Ava remembers thinking how crazy it was that her brain could shut out the trauma as if it never happened. Eventually, as the woman got older, she started having flashbacks and nightmares of her time held in captivity. She would see the most random things and suddenly be hit with a wave of remembering. It's proof that while the brain can do its best to protect us from harm, harm eventually finds a way in. One way or another, it always finds a way in.

Paul Summers. Ava is hit by her own wave of remembering. Paul Summers – one of the many foster dads she had throughout her childhood. Paul Summers – with his beady little eyes and mustache that curled at the edges. Summers – the man who raped Ava countless times. Paul Summers – the man who lay brain dead at the bottom of the steps.

"Paul–" Ava can't bring herself to say his full name. As if saying it would make this all somehow very, very real.

"Paul Summers," Lucy replies, "You didn't really forget about him, did you?"

Ava has tuned Lucy out. She's on a malfunctioning rollercoaster going backward. The rollercoaster is taking her through every nook and cranny of her childhood. Ava is praying for these memories to be false but the lump in her throat suggests what she knows to be true. This was real life. This was her life. Her old life.

"You pushed him down the steps," Lucy interjects, "If I remember correctly, you pushed him and then immediately called me to clean up the mess."

ng up blank.

"No," Ava whispers.

"Yes, Ava."

Ava wills herself to remember. She remembers Lucy being at the Summers' house. It was late into the night. Paul Summers had finished an entire bottle of Johnie Walker whiskey. That was always his favorite. Ava knew what was coming for her that night. It would start with a knock at the door. Paul would try to sweetly coax Ava into his bedroom. When that didn't work, he would yank her arm and drag her down the hall into his room. It didn't matter how much she tried to kick and scream. It always ended the same. It always ended with Paul's big beer belly on top of Ava, making it hard for her to breathe. Ava called Lucy that night, begging her to help her escape. Begging her to help her sneak out of the house before Paul was too deep into his whiskey. They were almost down the staircase when he found them. There was a confrontation, but Ava can't remember the details. Everything is coming up blank.

What is clear as day is the image of Paul Summers lying

motionless at the bottom of the steps. She remembers Lucy

telling her to go back into bed and pretend like she's asleep.

She remembers Lucy telling her that Mrs.Summers would

be home from her night shift as a nurse bright and early in

the morning. All she had to do was pretend to sleep. Ava

remembers shutting her eyes so tight she was sure she

would be blind by the time she woke up.

"You didn't mean to hurt him, Ava," Lucy

continues, "But that doesn't exactly hold up in court, does

it?"

"No. I didn't hurt him. I couldn't have hurt him."

Ava looks to Lucy for an answer. It's an answer she knows

she doesn't want to hear.

"Please don't make me go to the police with this,"

Lucy continues, "I fear you wouldn't do too well in jail."

"No. I didn't do it," Ava repeats, "I know I didn't do

it."

"But do you know that?" Lucy asks in a taunting tone.

The truth is Ava doesn't know. Her memory has failed her. All these years, she's shut this out. She buried it so deep that not even her subconscious mind can recall it. Her mind must have designed it to be that way. To bury it so deep she can't be haunted by it. She wouldn't have hurt him. She doesn't have it in her to hurt someone. Ava was born with her mother's kindness. She was not born with the DNA to harm someone. But can she be sure of that? Was it an accident gone wrong? All these questions are flying a mile a minute inside Ava's brain.

Ava steps closer to Lucy so they're almost an arm's length away. She does something that surprises even her. She faces it.

"Go ahead and tell the police," Ava says, her expression turning to anger.

"Oh, I'm sure you don't want me to do that. You need to think clearly here, Ava."

"It's your word against mine." Ava continues, "A high school dropout turned hotel cleaning lady versus an accomplished architect with multiple degrees. I'll take those odds any day."

"Ava…" Lucy says. It almost comes out as a plea.

"This conversation is over. Your endless threats are over. The fight is finally over."

This time, Ava does not wait for Lucy's response. She spins around on her heels and marches into the house. Her house. Her property. Her old life. Her new life. And everything in between. She's here for it all and she sure as hell isn't going anywhere.

TESSA

"What do you want to know?" Doctor Carmichael

asks. He's sitting across from Tessa at the big farm table. They both have a large serving of salmon on their plates with colorfully cooked carrots.

"Everything. Don't leave out anything." Tessa says as she takes a bite of the fish. She's cooked for them every night since moving (temporarily) into Doctor Carmichael's place. She's started to become obsessed with cooking. Like writing, it's given her a chance to be alone with just her and her thoughts.

"Well, I have a daughter. I'm not sure if you knew that."

Tessa almost chokes on her fish. A daughter? No, she definitely did not know that. He must have left that out. Then again, most of their conversations have focused solely on Tessa's life and how to help her overcome her inner demons. They've been very one-sided conversations, Tessa is just now realizing.

"Oh," Tessa replies, "I did not know that."

"I'm sorry. I should have told you. I just –" Doctor Carmichael reaches across the table and places his hand over Tessa's hand, "I just didn't want to overwhelm you. It's been so nice—these moments of just you and I. Of us getting to know one another and seeing if this could be something. I didn't want to tell you until I was sure this was something. I should have told you sooner. I'm sorry."

Tessa should be upset that he hid this part of his life from her, but she's not. This is something. He confirmed it. Tessa has been so confident that this is something, but she wasn't sure if he felt the same. How could Tessa be mad? She finally has something and she's not letting it slip through her hands this time. Plus, she's sure she could make a decent stepmother. Yes, she's getting quite ahead of herself, but she can't help it. This is more than something. This is it. Her search is over. She finally found it. After all these years of looking, she finally found him.

"Tessa, please. Please just say something," Doctor Carmichael continues.

Tessa places her fork down. She stands up and grabs Doctor Carmichael's arm and leads him into the bedroom.

AVA

Ava is lying wide awake in bed as Tommy is next to her, deep into his REM sleep. He's breathing heavily. He seems at ease, quite the opposite of how Ava is feeling right now. Tommy came over for dinner and Ava asked him to stay the night. She needed the distraction. She needed to forget that the standoff with Lucy Gonzalez had ever happened. Tommy was a welcome distraction, for sure. But the memories are all too eager to creep back in as soon as Ava has a free moment to herself.

Ava is no longer doubtful that night with Paul Summers happened. She knows that night was real. She just can't seem to remember the details of that night. It's as if she's trying to solve some jigsaw puzzle, but half of the pieces are missing. They're just out of reach. Until she can finish the puzzle, she knows the dread will gnaw at her and keep coming back for more. Tommy noticed something was off during dinner. He asked Ava if she was ok. She brushed it off as just being tired. While Ava would love nothing more than to tell Tommy, she can't. Not until she finishes the puzzle. And this isn't some 500-piece puzzle. This puzzle is thousands of tiny, minuscule pieces. She better get working…

LUCY

He's coming here tomorrow. He's going to handle it. I told him I was out of options. I gave it my all and yet nothing seemed to stick. He said he was disappointed that I couldn't handle it myself. I wish he would had chosen any other word besides disappointed. Shit, I wish he would have just been angry. That would have felt better, somehow. But disappointing him was a sucker punch. I didn't just let him down. I let us down. But he'll make it better. He always has a way of making it better. He'll be here tomorrow to make it all better. Now I can finally sleep knowing this will all be over by tomorrow.

AVA

James Taylor is playing from Ava's phone as she and Tommy shuck ears of corn. Ava was adamant that they have corn for the barbeque this afternoon. The barbeque was Tommy's idea. He wanted to cheer Ava up. She still hasn't been able to shake the dread that seems to be circling in on her since her conversation with Lucy yesterday. Tommy has done his best not to ask and Ava has assured him she will share when she's ready. Or maybe she won't.

She hasn't thought that far ahead.

Right now, Ava is focusing all her attention on the barbeque and making sure they have enough food. Tommy asked Ava if Tessa could join today. Of course, Ava said yes. While Tessa and Ava didn't exactly get off to the best start, Ava knows Tessa is an extension of Tommy. She will mend the fence with Tessa if it's the last thing she does. This is important to Tommy, so it's important to her.

TESSA

I initially didn't want to go when Tommy invited me to the barbeque. But then, I remembered I had to get my journal and a few other things I left behind at the house. That is, if she hasn't already thrown them out. I'm sure she's tossed out my stray belongings without giving it so much as a second thought. When Tommy told me he'd striked up a connection with her, I had to restrain myself from puking. Her? Of all people? Tommy reminded me that

he was less than thrilled with the person I'd decided to

date. So, it was only fair. I would come to the barbeque and

do my absolute best to be nice. If not nice, at least polite.

It's a speech he'd given me countless of other times before I

was set to meet his new beau. Each girl I met seemed to get

progressively worse. As I've said, Tommy has terrible taste

in women. The way Tommy talks about Ava seems different,

though. He's all in on her. Blind to the earth-shattering

pain his heart could face should this all come tumbling

down. Blind love. The worst kind. I know this because it's

the exact same way I feel about Alex. All in. I begged

Tommy to let me bring Alex to the barbeque but Tommy

said that wasn't a good idea. Not this time. He wanted me

to have time with Ava, just the two of us. It didn't matter

anyway, as Alex had to work this afternoon. I look forward

to catching him up on everything tonight. I'm cooking filet

mignon for dinner. I've gotten quite good at cooking the

perfect steak. Betty Crocker, eat your heart out.

LUCY

He didn't send me any details. He just gave me the time to be there. That was it. It was like we were just two colleagues preparing for a business meeting. I guess, in a way, this is a business meeting. However, I'm confident there will be no formalities or niceties this time. Not when the biggest deal of all is on the table.

AVA

The screen door of the house slams shut.

Ava and Tommy are snapped out of their lull. Tommy is covered in baking powder. He's been baking all morning, attempting to make the perfect seven-tier chocolate cake. He wants to try and replicate the seven-tiered cake he once had when visiting this tiny island in Southern Maryland.

Tommy smiles at Ava, "Must be Tessa."

Ava does her best to give him a reassuring smile. This is it—showtime. She will be kind to Tessa no matter how much it pains her. She will try to forget the fact that Tessa was squatting on this property, refusing to leave. She will forget that Ava had to give Tessa a hefty amount of money to vacate the property. She will even forget that Tessa shoved her. Clean slate. That was the agreement.

"Tommy?" Tessa calls out from down the hallway.

"In here!" Tommy yells back.

Within seconds, Tessa comes waltzing into the kitchen. She's wearing a bright yellow sundress with an off-white peacoat. Her hair is combed back into a slicked-back bun. She looks different. Put together. She looks good, Ava must admit. She also put on some weight since Ava last saw her. She looks healthy.

"Brother dearest!" Tessa says. She goes in for the hug but recoils when she sees the powder that covers Tommy's apron.

"Smart choice," Tommy jokes.

Tessa turns to Ava. Here goes nothing, Ava thinks.

Tessa hands Ava a large bouquet of sunflowers. 'Are you fucking kidding me' is all Ava can think. Of all flowers. Really?

Ava does her best to accept the gift graciously. "Thank you, they're beautiful."

"Thank you for having me. I'm looking forward to starting fresh with you." Tessa replies.

"Likewise," Ava says, "What can we get you to drink? We have water, Sprite, Diet Coke, soda water, and freshly squeezed lemonade."

Ava made sure this barbeque was alcohol-free. Tommy said it wasn't necessary. He said Tessa should get used to being in scenarios where she would be around alcohol. That may be true but Ava wasn't willing to risk it—not today.

"Oh! I'll try the lemonade. Sounds lovely."

Ava does her best to stifle a laugh. This prim and proper Tessa will take some getting used to, that's for sure.

Ava grabs a stack of plates and napkins from the china cabinet. "I'll be right back. I'm going to set the table outside."

"Here! Let me help!" Tessa says, jumping to attention.

"Thanks. If you could grab the stack of those plates there, that would be great."

Tessa obliges and grabs a handful of preppy pastel plates. Tessa peeks behind one of the shelves in the china cabinet. She grabs her peacock-covered journal and tucks it into the breast pocket of her peacoat.

Tessa follows Ava to the outdoor deck. Ava is lining up the plates and making sure everything looks just right.

"You've outdone yourself, Ava," Tessa says as she places the stack of plates on the table. "Even the tablecloth matches the decor!"

"Thank you, Tessa." Ava says, letting her name hang in the air for a few delayed seconds, "And thank you for coming today. I know it means a lot to your brother that you're here."

"And what about you?"

"Me?"

"Yeah. Are you happy to see me?" Tessa asks bullishly.

Ava sits down on one of the chairs, visibly debating this question. Her gut reaction would be, 'hell no.' However, Ava knows she could never say that. The honest answer is she's unsure how she feels about Tessa being here. Part of her is terrified of seeing her again after everything went down the way it did. But the other genuine part of her wants to get to know Tessa. Tessa has known Tommy the longest and has been there throughout every stage of his life. Ava knows she hasn't even scratched the surface of Tommy's past. She's also pretty sure Tommy will never reveal everything to her. Not because he doesn't want to but because he won't be able to. She knows it better than anyone that some memories aren't meant to be reopened. They're not meant to be poked and prodded at. They're simply meant to be left as is.

"I am happy to see you. I agree that it will be good for the two of us to start over. To turn a fresh page."

"I'm very protective of my brother, so you can understand my shock when he told me the two of you were together."

"I understand."

"Tommy is the only person in my family who truly sees me." Tessa continues, "He knows what my deepest, darkest fears are, just like he knows how to make me laugh at just the right moment. I was plopped into a life that wasn't necessarily mine. At times, I was forced to do things I didn't want to do. Everyone in our family liked swimming in the ocean, so I had to like swimming in the ocean. Everyone loved board games, so I had to learn to love them. Tommy knew I was afraid of sharks, just like he knew I was a terrible cheater with any board game. He saw me as exactly who I was and never asked for anything more. He never once tried to form me into the person he thought I should be. He met me where I was. Does that make sense?"

"It does – because that's exactly how he is with me. He meets me where I am and never asks for anything more. It's a beautiful thing to be seen. Isn't it?" Ava replies.

"It really is."

"You and I are going to be okay. It will take some time and we may not be the best of friends, but we'll be okay."

"You think so?"

"I know so," Ava declares, "Because we love the same person. We are bonded by this invisible thread woven together by our love for Tommy."

"You love him!?" Tessa asks. She's almost giddy with childlike excitement.

"I do. I really do." Ava says. "I know it sounds ridiculous, given I've known him for less than two weeks. This feeling in my heart is not lust; it's pure love. I know I must sound crazy. I can't believe I'm even admitting this to you! "

"Have you told him?"

Ava shakes her head, "Not yet. I was planning to tonight, actually."

"Love who?" A man's voice asks.

Ava and Tessa simultaneously turn around.

Ava drops the stack of pastel plates she's holding. The plates hit the deck in what feels like slow motion. The pieces shatter around Ava's feet, almost like the little speckles of sea glass she used to collect at the beach.

Ava is as pale as a ghost. Scratch that. She makes the palest ghost look tan.

"Ava! Are you okay?" Tessa shrieks. There are still a few shards of glass in Ava's hands that have caused some blood to drip from her palms.

"Dad?" Ava says, not taking her eyes off the figure that stands before her. The man has a thick beard that covers most of his face. Even with the beard, Ava is sure it's him. You don't forget those eyes. That nose. It's all too similar to her nose. She's always hated her nose. And now those eyes are looking right back at her. Jeff McGready's eyes are piercing right through her heart.

Lucy Gonzalez steps forward from behind Jeff McGready's shadow, "Why don't we all go somewhere we can talk?"

"Dad?" It's all Ava can seem to spit out. It's as if saying Dad enough times would be the magic formula to wake her up from this dream.

Tessa looks back and forth from Ava to this man like she's at some sort of tennis match, "I don't get it. What's going on?"

"You've grown into such a beautiful woman, Tessa," Jeff says, ignoring her question.

Tessa looks at him with pure confusion, "I'm sorry, have we met before?"

"Something like that," Jeff replies almost mockingly.

"It can't be. You're alive?" Ava chokes out in disbelief. "I can't —"

"I know you have a lot of questions. I'm hoping I

can answer them for you. I know it all doesn't make sense right now but I promise you it's really me. I've missed you so damn much, my Ako."

Ako. Those three letters twist the dagger securely in Ava's heart. Those three letters confirm it all to be true. Only her father called her Ako. It was their secret little nickname.

"Where is mom!?" Ava sputters out. A wave of hopefulness washes over her face. If her dad is standing here in the flesh, surely her mom is here also. Maybe she's going to pop out of the tree and surprise her, Ava thinks. Her mom always loved to play practical jokes on people.

Jeff shakes his head and lowers his eyes. The wave of hope instantaneously disappears from Ava's face.

"But how? How are you here?" Ava whispers.

Tessa is studying every inch of Jeff McGready's body. She's met him somewhere, but where? She can't seem to place him.

"I can't stay long. In fact, I really shouldn't be here at all, but –" Jeff clears his throat, "Lucy called me, and I knew what had to be done. I didn't want us to reunite like this. All my life, I debated on whether seeing me again would help you gain the closure I knew you desperately needed. But I feared it would only hurt you, especially because I can't stay. I knew how unfair it would be to return to your life knowing I had to leave again. I knew that would rip open the wound again. I couldn't risk that."

"Wait, this man is your father?" Tessa interjects, only to be met with silence. She's catching up, but she's just a few steps behind.

"Time is really of the essence here. Which is why it's important you listen closely to what I'm about to tell you. I need you to do that for me. Can you do that for me, Ako?"

Ava is nodding her head yes, not really knowing what she's agreeing to. All she can think of is the fact that her dad is alive. He's here in the flesh. It's almost as if

seeing him has made her revert back to her childlike self.

She's always been a daddy's girl. She'd do anything her dad

wanted or asked of her. Even now, after all these years.

That feeling doesn't go away.

"Ava, you can't sell this land."

"Why?"

"Because there are bodies buried here." Lucy

interjects before Jeff can reply.

———————

LUCY

It's not my job to make it all make sense. That's

Jeff's job, really. Although I'm fairly confident he doesn't

know how to make any of this make sense. I presume he'll

do what he always does. He'll take the easy way out. He'll

lie, cheat, and do just about anything else he can think of to

make sure he comes out on top. He's a blubbering mess and

we don't exactly have time for that. He needs to get to the freaking point. He's left it upon me to have to spell it all out for them. Make sense out of the senseless.

"Holy shit," Tessa says, and not just because of what Lucy has just said. Tessa is just now realizing who Lucy Gonzalez is. She is just now putting it together that Lucy Gonzalez is the very same woman who gave her the keys to this property. Lucy is the same woman she met outside her AA meeting almost a year ago. Lucy Gonzalez is the woman who approached her with the deal of a lifetime.

"Bodies?" Ava asks. "I'm sorry, did you say bodies?"

"Lives were not meant to be lost. I want that to be very clear. It was supposed to be cut and dry. It was strictly supposed to be a transactional operation, and we were supposed to know as little as possible. It was better that way. For everyone." Lucy continues, ignoring Ava. "If we had any inkling that we would be getting involved with one of the largest trafficking organizations in the world, we would have never agreed. The money jaded us. We didn't ask enough questions after seeing the money coming in. We were all too quick to turn a blind eye."

Tessa and Ava look at each other with sheer terror in their eyes.

Lucy continues, "Things got…complicated. More shipments of girls were getting routed here. We couldn't handle the volume. What was supposed to be a brief pit stop for a few hours turned into extended overnight stays. It became all too much for us to handle."

Tessa is the first to process the words coming out of Lucy's mouth. Her confusion quickly turns to panic.

Tessa grabs Ava's arm, "We're going to the police. C'mon, Ava. Don't say another word to them. We're going to the police."

Ava is too stunned to speak. Her two feet remain firmly planted on the ground.

"No. Don't call the police." Ava orders.

"Ava, please! We need to get out of here. Now!" Tessa pleads.

"Please don't do this. Don't make me kill my two daughters." Jeff says.

"Daughters!?" Ava and Tessa both reply in unison.

Jeff looks at Ava and then to Tessa. It's a look of a father's admiration. "Yes, my two beautiful daughters. Look at you two. You each look so much like your mothers."

"You're not my dad. That's not possible." Tessa is shaking her head vigorously like she's a broken bobblehead.

"I am. Your mother was a wonderful woman. We met – well, we met during this whole thing." Jeff motions to the land around them as if this one motion can sum up any further explanation. "The minute she stepped off the boat, she took my breath away."

"Don't you dare." Tessa growls through her teeth.

"She had the most beautiful golden blonde hair and bronzed skin. She had a birthmark that ran up the side of her shoulder and towards her neck. On anyone else it would have looked ridiculous, but on your mother it was just stunning."

"Oh my god," Ava replies. She remembers. Of course she remembers her. The woman who appeared countless times in her dreams, looking at her through the sand dollar mirror, begging her to remember.

Now Tessa is the one frozen in place. It's her mother. She could never forget that iconic birthmark. She could never forget the woman who appeared countless times in her dreams, looking at her through the sand dollar mirror, begging her to remember. If that's true, that means the man standing in front of her is also the man from her dreams. The man whom she tried to run away from and the very same man who visited her on the swing set when she was at the foster home.

"What did you do to her!" Tessa screams. It's a scream that rattles your insides. It echoes across the entire bay only to be met with terrifying silence.

TESSA

The crash that comes after a high should have prepared me for this. It should have taken the blow out of this just a bit. But no. Nothing could have prepared me for this. My very first thought was how happy Alex would be. I finally found the thing that I'd been unknowingly running from. The thing that imprisoned me. And now, here I was. Facing it. As if I had any choice in the matter. Tommy will make it all better. I just need to get to Tommy. Where the hell is Tommy?

"I know you think I'm this awful man, but that's not true. At least, that's not the whole truth. I'm a good man who has done some pretty awful things. But I'm not a bad man. I had Lucy keep a close eye on the two of you. I helped at a distance whenever I could." Jeff takes a step forward, "Ava, I was the one who called Archer Architects to make sure you got the job when I found out you were interviewing. I used my connections to ensure you got paid the highest salary an entry-level worker could get."

Ava is going to be sick. He'd been keeping tabs on her all this time. How did she not know? She worked so hard to land her job at Archer Architects. She prepared endlessly. Ava remembers when she got the call from the firm's president congratulating her on landing the job. She'd been surprised, especially given how competitive the interview process had been. She'd been just as surprised when they told her the hefty salary she'd be pulling in as an entry-level architect. Now it all makes sense. She never did earn the job, did she? It's just another piece in the unsolvable puzzle that seems to be her life.

"Tessa, I sent Lucy to bring you to this house when I found out you were living out of a suitcase. I made sure you had a roof over your head. I know optically it doesn't seem like much, but I promise you I never let anything or anyone harm you." Jeff clears his throat and continues, "I even had Lucy check in on you both at the Catholic foster home. I wanted to be sure my daughters had someone they could lean on. Someone trustworthy who I knew would protect them."

"Mom... where was mom?" Ava blurts out. It's the only thing she can think of. Her mother would never have let this happen. Never. Her mother was a real-life angel who would have fought tooth and nail to protect Ava from this madness.

Jeff takes another step closer to Ava. His eyes soften. Ava's heart drops. "I loved your mother. I loved her so very much. She just wouldn't let it go. I begged her to turn a blind eye, but she kept doubling down. She was threatening to expose the whole operation. If this got out, they would take out our entire family. I had no choice. I had to save you. I had to make sure you would always be safe. She left me no choice. Ava, please. You have to believe me!" Jeff is choking through his tears.

"Oh my god," Ava says, "You killed her, didn't you?" She's trying to suck in air but all she can feel is her windpipe closing in. She's starting to see stars.

"You. You were there that night. When you helped me out of the car," Ava is now pointing aggressively at Lucy, "I was covered in blood and you carried me out of the car. I always wondered why you were there that night. I never understood how you could've been at the scene so fast."

Ava forces herself to remember that night. She's tried so hard to push it out when it has threatened to penetrate the steel gates of her mind. The blood. The buckets and buckets of blood that surrounded Ava in the car. Someone was crying. Ava forces herself to go there. To dive deep within the darkness. The person crying was her mom. Her mom was crying out for help.

"She was still alive. When the car hit the tree, my mom was still alive. You killed her after the fact." It's not a question this time because Ava knows the answer. Her entire life, she's been in pursuit of the answers, only to have them flying at her at warp speed.

"Oh my God," Tessa says.

"You deliberately hit the tree. You staged it as an accident." Ava continues, the answers pouring out of her before she can swallow them back down. "You staged your own death, didn't you? But how?"

"A friend at the coroner's office owed me a favor," Jeff says, making no attempt to deny Ava's accusations. "Just like my attorney at Thompkins Bay law firm owed me a favor. As silent investors of our operation, they protected me so I wouldn't out them. I did the dirty work while they received a generous amount of kickbacks. I was the fall guy but they were crucial in making it all go away." Jeff is almost laughing now, "You know, it really isn't as hard as you would think to stage your own death."

"Stop it!" Ava screams. The noise causes a group of birds to fly off in the distance.

"Your mother ruined everything! She went to the Feds and revealed it all. She told them what she suspected I was doing. They were closing in on me. If the Feds found me first, the bad people would undoubtedly have come after you and your mother. They wanted to make sure anyone who was associated with our operation would be silenced for good. I had to act fast. The only way I saw a way out was to make it all look like an accident. They would leave you alone if they knew I was dead. Your mother would have outed the whole operation and they would have killed you both out of retaliation. There was no other way. Don't you see?"

"I don't believe you. You're a liar. The Feds would have protected me. They would have protected mom."

"Maybe for a little, yes. But they would have found you both. These are very bad people, Ava. They wouldn't have stopped until they found you both. Not even the Feds could have protected you from them."

"And what about Lucy? How is she still standing here?"

"They had no idea about Lucy. She was another silent investor, so to speak."

Ava is shaking her head in disbelief. This can't be happening. This has to be a dream. This has to be a very bad nightmare. If only she could just wake up now.

"It was the only way, Ava! You must understand that!" Jeff says, screaming. He's desperate for Ava to understand. "I was protecting you! I know it's hard to see right now but you must believe that!"

"So instead, you chose the most cowardly option of all. You killed your wife, left your daughter parentless, and jetted off to a wonderful new life in the Caribbean or wherever the hell you've been holing up. Why didn't you just do us all a favor and kill yourself, too?"

"You needed me." Jeff says in a voice that sounds unrecognizable. It's a low, threatening tone. He turns his attention toward Tessa, "You both needed me. I had to watch over you both to make sure you would always be safe from harm. Why are you not understanding this!? It's the truth!"

Ava approaches her father like a lion approaching their prey. Her tears make it hard for her to see in front of her, but she presses on. One foot in front of the other. She's facing this.

"We never needed you. Not then and certainly not now. You're a killer."

"I'm not!"

"You killed her! My mother!" Ava lets out a gut-wrenching wail. "And then you just left me! You skipped town and left me like I was just some forgotten luggage!"

―――――――――

AVA

As fast as the information was coming at me, it all felt like slow motion. Like I was moving through molasses. Wanna know the weirdest part? I somehow subconsciously felt something like this would happen. Not to this extent, obviously. No one could have guessed this. If I really thought about it, I was always waiting for the other shoe to drop and I never quite understood why. I created such a safe and cushiony life for myself in London. I had everything I needed. Yet there were times when the dread felt like it would eat me alive. That's why I got into running.

I would quite literally run from the dread that threatened to blow up my idealistic life. I chased after the life I was never granted when I was younger. But I somehow knew deep down that this was coming. It was only a matter of time. I guess that's what happens when you try to outrun the wave. It turns into a damn tsunami.

JEFF

They're not understanding. Especially Ava. Not like I assumed she would. Ava inherited my stubbornness, after all. They're asking me why I did it, as if there's one simple explanation to it all. But that's like asking why good people do bad things. The answer is far too complicated to put into words. The most simple answer I can give them is I got desperate. Really desperate. I was behind on my property taxes and the bank was threatening foreclosure. My marriage to Donna was not in a good place. I was desperate to get us back on track. I knew if I lost the land,

she would leave me for good. I couldn't let that happen. It

was my friend Gerold Finley at Thompkins Bay Law Firm

who first approached me with the opportunity. He, of

course, couldn't get his hands dirty with any of it. They

were looking for someone willing to be more hands on. I

said yes because what else was I to do? I knew I was doing

a bad thing but I was surprised at just how easy it was to

disassociate. There was still some goodness inside of me

when this whole thing started. I'm not exactly sure when I

crossed the invisible threshold of good versus evil, but it

was probably right around the time when the first girl died.

I was in too deep. I reached the point of no return. I knew

that and I was okay with that. Everything after that was

pretty cut and dry. All the decisions I made after that were

solely made to protect myself and my family at all costs.

Plus, with all the extra money I was raking in, my wife was

happier than ever. I knew she would never leave me once

she had more than enough fun money to go around. We were happy again. Finally. But happiness is fleeting, isn't it? People get greedy and greediness is what evil feeds off of. It all came tumbling down quicker than a house of cards. I had to act fast. I had to save my precious Ako. Why is she not understanding that?

———————

"Are you even sorry?" Ava asks, interrupting Jeff's thoughts.

Before Ava can hear the answer to his question, she's hit with another wave of remembering. She's back on the steps with Lucy and Paul Summers. There's an altercation on the top of the steps. Paul grabs Lucy's wrist, shaking her hard. It happens in the blink of an eye. Lucy shoves Paul down the steps. He has nothing to hold onto as his head smacks the bottom step. Lucy is grabbing Ava's hand, leading her back into her bed. She's forcing Ava's eyes closed. She's telling her not to open them until morning.

"You pushed him!" Ava says, facing Lucy again. She's frantic now, trying to put the pieces of the puzzle in their correct places. "You pushed him, and you were going to blame it on me."

"You were the one who called me asking for help," Lucy replies. Lucy doesn't need clarification. She knows exactly what Ava is referring to. "If you didn't like the help you received, you should never have asked in the first place. I made him go away, didn't I?"

"You're evil. You're utterly evil." Ava says through more tears. The information coming at her has been too much. The dam she's meticulously built up has finally broken. Lucy killed Paul Summers and made it seem like a drunken accident. If she's capable of that, who knows what else she's capable of.

"Let's go, Tessa. Get inside." Ava is now the one who is desperate to get Tessa and her back to safety.

"What did you do to my mother?" Tessa growls, ignoring Ava. She's slowly circling in on Jeff.

Before Tessa can approach further, Jeff grabs a gun from his back pocket. He points the gun in Tessa's direction, halting her from moving any closer.

"Don't come any closer," Jeff warns.

"What did you do to my mother!" Tessa is screaming as loud as she can. "What did you do to her!?"

Before Ava can process what is happening, Tessa is running toward Jeff at full speed. Right before she reaches him, Jeff presses down on the trigger.

Tessa falls instantly to the ground. It happens so quickly that, for a second, Ava doubts if it even happened at all. But looking at Tessa lying motionless on the ground confirms it to be true. Jeff shot Tessa. Her father shot her sister.

"Tessa!" Ava screams.

"You fucking shot her!" Lucy yells at Jeff.

"What else was I supposed to do? She was going to attack me! Fuck!" Jeff screams back.

"Tessa!" Ava screams again.

Tessa lets out a moan. She tries to stand up but falls back down. She's grabbing at her chest. She reaches into her peacoat and pulls out the peacock-covered journal. The bullet is lodged smack dab in the middle of the journal. Tessa is looking down at the journal in disbelief. She shouldn't be alive. That journal saved her life.

Ava needs to help Tessa. She turns to run toward Tessa, but Jeff cocks the gun at Ava. "Don't move! Fuck! If you both would do as I say, this wouldn't have happened! Why won't you listen to your father!? Look, I didn't mean to shoot her! I –"

Before Jeff can finish that sentence, he's tumbling face-first into the grass. The wind has been knocked out of him as Tommy is pinning him to the ground. Jeff's gun goes flying in Tessa's direction. Tessa winces in pain as she scrambles on the ground for the gun. She grabs the gun firmly with both of her hands.

"Get the fuck off of me!" Jeff yells at Tommy.

Jeff continues to squirm under the weight of Tommy's muscular body. Jeff snaps his elbow back, making contact with Tommy's nose. Tommy instinctively grabs his nose and lets loose on his grip on Jeff. Blood is instantaneously covering Tommy's hands. His nose is definitely broken.

Jeff stands up and faces his two daughters. He starts to walk toward Tessa but she cocks the gun right at him.

"Whoa! Whoa, Tessa. It's okay. Relax. It's okay," Jeff repeats. "We will figure this all out. Just put down the gun. It will all be okay. We're family."

———————

AVA

All these thoughts are rushing through me at once:

My dad killed my mom.

My dad ran a sex trafficking ring.

My dad raped a teenage girl.

My dad has another daughter.

My dad is Tessa's dad.

My dad is alive.

My dad is a monster.

My dad has to die.

TESSA

All these thoughts are rushing through me at once:

My dad killed my mom.

My dad ran a sex trafficking ring.

My dad raped my mother when she was just a teenager.

My dad is Ava's dad.

My dad is alive.

My dad is a monster.

My dad has to die.

LUCY

Only one thought crosses my mind:

Jeff McGready has to die.

"Don't move!" Tessa says. She has the gun pointed directly at Jeff's head.

"Tess, hand me the gun," Tommy demands. His entire face is covered in blood. "You don't want to do this."

"He fucking shot me! He's a killer. He deserves to die!

"Tessa, Tommy's right," Ava says calmly. "He's a killer, but you don't have to be. He is not us. He is not our family. You are my family."

Tessa directs her attention to Ava. She's desperate for help. She's desperate for her older half-sister to step in and take control. A sister she never knew existed until this very moment. Ava is looking back at her with those helpless, deep blue eyes. Tessa must protect her. She must protect her sister at all costs. She must protect her family.

"Why did you kill her?" Tessa asks, turning back to face Jeff. Her tone is softer now. She's defeated. She never knew she was capable of feeling all these emotions at once.

Jeff is crying again. The tears seem to come erratically. "I didn't kill her! I was so in love with her. I would never have sent her away. They sent her away, and I couldn't do anything about it. They sent her away, and I couldn't protect her."

"Who sent her away?" Tessa demands, ignoring Jeff's hysterics. "Who!?"

"I did," Lucy interjects, "I sent her away when I knew Jeff was getting in too deep with her. He was getting sloppy. Making mistakes. We weren't in the type of business where we could afford mistakes. We certainly couldn't afford any distractions. She needed to disappear. How was I to know the ship was going to catch fire? How was I to know that the ship would burst into flames?"

"You killed her?" Tessa asks, now facing Lucy. "You killed her!"

"Tessa, hand me the gun. Please, I'm begging you." Tommy says.

Tessa shakes her head, ignoring her brother. "How many bodies are buried here?"

It's a question directed toward Lucy. Tessa is now eerily calm.

"I'm unsure. Six. Maybe seven."

"Six!?" Ava screams. "Oh my God!"

"Some of the girls came to us in really bad shape. Dehydrated, malnourished. You name it. We did our best to help them. We really did. But for some of them, it was just too late. They got to us too late."

"How can you live with yourselves? How do you wake up every single day knowing what you did?" Ava asks.

"Ava, life is woven together by an invisible string of good and bad moments. I taught you that at a young age, didn't I? You hope that the good outweighs the bad. You really do. But most of the time, you can only hope the good cancels out the bad." Jeff says. The look in his eyes makes it seem like he truly believes his words. "I've worked hard to repent for my sins. Every single day, I work to repent my sins. And while I know it may never be enough to make up for what I've done, it has to mean something, doesn't it?

"Tessa, I–" Is all Lucy can get out before the loud bang of the gun goes off. Ava's eyes are on Tessa, watching her slowly release her finger from the trigger.

———————

AVA

The ringing in my ears is too loud to make out what Tommy is saying. He's yelling at Tessa, but I can't quite seem to process the words. I can't take my eyes off my dad. Lucy's blood is splattered on his t-shirt, making it look almost tie-dye-like. My dad is staring right back at me. Our eyes are locked in unison. He says nothing. He doesn't even look down at Lucy, who is face down on the ground in a pool of blood. His eyes are only on me. He does something that sends a chill down my spine. I swear I see him wink at me. He winked at me right before I'm being escorted away by someone with a police badge. Right before he's face down on the ground in handcuffs. A final moment between just the two of us. Father and daughter.

Three months Later

Ava reaches over and pulls open the window shade. There's something romantic about staring out into the black of the night from thirty thousand feet up in the air.

Ava reaches over and caresses Tommy's thigh. His head is resting on her shoulder as he sleeps. Ava just can't get enough of watching him sleep.

At first, she was apprehensive about inviting Tommy along with her to London. She was afraid of what kind of Pandora's box it would open up. After thinking about it a bit more, she knew it was the right thing to do. She wanted Tommy to see London through her eyes. To experience what has been Ava's life for the past fifteen-plus years. Sure, there would be hard moments. There would even be places and things she'll reluctantly have to revisit. But none of that matters as long as Tommy would be there, holding her hand through it all.

A few weeks ago, Max called, asking for a second chance. He told Ava he'd made a mistake. He remained confident that the two of them could work through this. He told Ava he could forget all about her cheeky little rendezvous in Chestertown. Maybe he really did want a second chance, or maybe the joint bank account they previously shared had run dry. There'd been rumblings amongst Ava's friends that Max spent three straight nights at a casino, pissing away all his money. Max's parents cut him off completely. So yes, maybe he was still in love with Ava, or maybe he was in love with the nice piece of real estate she recently inherited. Either way, it didn't matter. Not anymore.

Ava reaches into her backpack and pulls out a letter. It's addressed to Ava from Tessa. Tessa has been sending letters weekly. She says it's really helped her keep her mind sharp. She wants to make sure she stays in a good head space while she's in there. Five years is a long time. Once

Lucy Gonzalez's family learned the extent of the crimes

Lucy committed, they agreed to reach a plea deal—a

diminished sentence for Tessa in agreement that the

Gonzalez name wouldn't be dragged through the media.

Patty didn't want another family to suffer the way many

others had at the hands of her mother. Ava felt bad leaving

on this two-week trip to London. She knows Tommy is a

bit uneasy about not getting to visit Tessa while they're

away. Luckily, Doctor Carmichael has been able to visit

Tessa every day since she arrived at Briar Penitentiary.

Sometimes twice a day.

Ava opens the letter:

Hey sis! HA, that still feels so weird to write. Maybe I'll

just stick with Ava for now if you're okay with it. I took a

yoga class today. The instructor was phenomenal! So

positive and inspirational. She told me if I practiced

enough and took enough classes, I could get certified to teach the classes myself one day. How cool would that be?!

Next time you visit, I'll show you a few of my favorite poses. I'm fairly good at tree pose, but I think that's mainly because I'm tall. I'm taking a pottery class tomorrow. I'm thinking of making you some pink plates. From what I can remember, you're in need of a new set. Have so much fun in London. Tommy will never admit this, but he quite fancies himself a cup of tea. He tries to be all manly with his black coffee, but he's not fooling anyone. Take him to get some tea. He will love you forever for it.

XO,

Tess

_____

AVA

It's weird thinking Tessa is sitting in the very same prison as our father. In a way, it almost makes this whole thing that much more painful. My father was served a life sentence. It was the right verdict. Of course it was. Although, it didn't make it any easier to hear. I had to not just grieve my father for a second time but also grieve for the father who was never really my father to begin with. That process is going to be a long and painful one. I'm not naive in that fact. If it weren't for Tommy calling the police, I'm confident my father would have found a way to slip through the cracks once again. Tommy called the police right before he ran out of the house to help. He saved our lives. If my father was going down, he was taking all of us down with him. That's just who he is. A coward until the very end. One thing that provides some comfort amidst all of this pain is knowing my mother's death was not in vain.

The Feds were already circling in on the entire operation but with my mother's help, they were able to narrow down the routes the shipments were being passed through. They were able to dismantle the entire operation from the very top. Because of my mother, the very bad people are now exactly where they should be: rotting in jail. Just like my father. My mother did not die in vain. My mother died a hero.

I quit my job at Archer Architects shortly after everything happened. Working at a place that had any affiliation with my father didn't feel right. I plan to start my own architectural firm, although I'm unsure where. Part of me wants to start fresh in a new town with new memories. The other part of me wants to stay put in Chestertown. A place that is so beautiful yet so very painful for me. I'm learning that there is always beauty in the pain if you look hard enough. I guess I have some more looking to do.

The property sold in less than twenty-four hours. I

had multiple bids, each one higher than the next. I decided

to go with an offer from the Maryland Preservatory Society.

The offer was less than half the amount of the other offers.

They plan to turn the seventy acres into a wildlife estuary.

The land will be protected from future development or

destruction. I had only two requests. I asked that they turn

the sunflower garden into a butterfly estuary. They say

butterflies are a sign from your loved ones that they are still

near and watching over you. I thought it would be a way to

memorialize the lives lost on the land, including my mother

and Tessa's mother. My second ask was that they stop

planting sunflowers. The society seemed more than willing

to oblige to these two requests. I moved in with Tommy until

I figure out my next move. Our next move. While I want to

live with him, I also want to ensure we give each other the

time needed to decompartmentalize everything. We both

just need a minute. I do make him take me to Lucky Shoe

Oyster Farm every morning. It's our happy place—just the two of us with our morning coffee. Time truly seems to stand still there.

Ava clutches her pearl necklace that sits on her collarbone. Her safety net. Only now, there is a second pearl. Tommy gave it to Ava as a promise. A promise that they would continue to build a life together. Each pearl would build onto the next until she had a full pearl necklace. He hoped she could eventually give it to their daughter one day if they were lucky enough to have a daughter. One day seems a lot closer than either of them ever thought. Ava clutches her flat stomach. She's not showing yet. It's far too early. She hasn't even told Tommy. She's not sure when she will. Maybe she will on this trip or when they're back home at the Lucky Shoe. One thing she is pretty sure of is that it's a girl.

Made in the USA
Middletown, DE
31 March 2025